ABOUT THE AUTHOR

Maggie Anderson is an Australian writer of romance, urban fantasy, supernatural crime thrillers and YA thrillers. She is currently working on a paranormal romance novel titled Wolf Blood which is the first book in the new series. Maggie resides in Brisbane, Queensland. You can find out more about her books at: www.m-anderson.com.au

Books by Maggie Anderson

Driving Me Crazy
Love's Twist of Fate
A Night of Passion
A Night of Passion Clean Edition

Paranormal Romance Series

Wolf Blood

Urban Fantasy Series
Writing as M. A. Anderson

Reece
Dark Legacy
Once Bitten
Soul Chaser

Driving ME Crazy

MAGGIE ANDERSON

Bella Luna Books
Australia

To all of the romance readers out there. Enjoy!

One

Peggy loved her job as a chauffeur. She was one of a select group of women in the male-dominated industry that had the opportunity to drive prestige cars and meet the most interesting people. High profiles, celebrities, and normal, everyday business types, and then of course, there were the weddings and school formals, which were always great fun. It was a charmed position and she was grateful.

She had previously worked in a mundane office job, finding it unbearable, and considered it to be a brain-numbing, nine to five grind that was going absolutely nowhere. But it had been a means to an end—paying the bills.

This morning, as Peggy drove to work, she had the distinct feeling that something was brewing. She couldn't quite put her finger on it, but *something* nonetheless. Normally, she felt the day was going to be great … her motto: *It's going to be a great day!* But not today, for some reason. Maybe she would have an awful client—an annoying celebrity type—arrogant and insensitive. She'd had her fair share of those before, and one in particular she hoped she would never lay eyes on again. Ever!

As she pulled her car into a parking space at the rear of the Crystal Limousine Company, Gary Taylor, her supervisor, rushed across the parking lot. When he got closer, he motioned for her to wind down the window.

Peggy pressed the button on the armrest, and the window glided into the door with a muted, mechanical hum. "Morning, Gary, what's the rush?" she asked, leaning her head out of the open window.

"Kent Reynolds is flying in today and he needs a driver," he said, pushing a piece of paper at her. "His manager just got off the phone."

Peggy shook her head. "Well, don't look at me. You remember what happened the last time I drove for him, don't you?"

Gary gave a heavy sigh. "It's been a year, I'm sure it's all forgotten. You're our best."

She glanced down and smiled. She was by no means conceited, but knew she was great at her job, and it was a good feeling to get the verbal recognition.

"I'm sure he's over it by now," Gary offered.

"*He's* over it? What about *me*? You do recall what he tried to do and then almost got me fired for it?"

"Of course I do. But we got it sorted with management and you're still here." He gave an unsure smile, small beads of perspiration forming across his wrinkled brow.

Peggy closed her eyes and took a deep breath. She had a soft spot for Gary; he'd been good to her and had given her a job when she suddenly found herself redundant. He was a good guy, like a second father to her. Peggy gave a huffy sigh. "Oh, all right." She shook her head and held out her hand for the piece of paper.

Gary's smile broadened. "Thanks, hon. And I do understand why you don't want to drive for him, but I really appreciate you doing it on such short notice."

Peggy pressed the button on the armrest and the window glided shut. She sighed again and pulled the keys from the ignition. Gary opened the door for her. "Thanks. How much are you paying me to endure Mr. Arrogant?" she asked, frowning at him as she stepped out of the car.

"You want hazard pay, do you?" Gary chuckled as he closed the car door.

Peggy wasn't smiling.

Her boss cleared his throat, the look of amusement disappearing from his face.

She glanced at the paper in her hand and her voice raised a decibel. "He's staying at the Palazzo Versace?"

"Yeah. Why not? He can afford it."

"What does he want this time?"

"Same as before. You're to stay in the suite with him, separate rooms of course, and do his bidding … I mean drive him wherever he wants to go." He gave her a sheepish smile.

"That's what I was afraid of." She pushed the paper into his hand. "It won't work. He's so … so exasperating. Can't Brenda do it? Or better yet, one of our male drivers?"

"She's driving Claudia Schiffer, and everyone else is booked. It's always like this at this time of the year."

"Why don't we just drive them around and pick them up like any other *normal* limousine company? Why do we have to spend 24/7 with these people? Don't you think I have anything better to do?"

"It's all part of the service. No one else offers it and the rich and famous love the convenience of having a driver on hand. You know that."

Peggy sighed again. "Yes, I know, but I really don't think I can do it. The last time I drove for him he was so rude and demanding. And he expected more than just a driver. He tried to…"

Gary waved it off. "His … his management has assured me nothing like that will happen again. Reynolds has been told it's a hands off policy, and he knows our female drivers aren't escorts."

"Well he didn't seem to understand that the last time he was here." She frowned at her boss.

"Please take the job, hon. I need you. And besides he tips well." Gary gave her a sideward glance.

"A five thousand dollar payment does not give him the right to thrust his sexual advances at me."

"No, it doesn't, but you could do with the extra cash, right? Please take the job. Gary nudged the paper toward her.

Peggy's gaze moved to the piece of notepaper in her boss's hand. She hadn't stayed at the Palazzo Versace Hotel before. It would be a treat she well deserved, having to endure Kent Reynolds for…

"How long?" she asked, folding her arms across her chest.

"What?"

"How long do I have to put up with the unbearable Mr. Arrogant?"

"Only seven days. Think you can handle it?"

Peggy snatched the paper from his hand. "Sure, especially when I'll be staying at the Versace hotel."

"Thank you." Gary's hands met in prayer. "All the flight details are there, he'll be flying into Brisbane…" he said, glancing at his watch, "in an hour. You'd better get a wriggle on. Don't want to be late."

"That was extremely short notice, wasn't it? Has the US finally wised up and exiled him out here for being an insufferable jerk?" Peggy was still uncomfortable about taking the job and having to spend seven days with the actor in his hotel suite.

"Yeah, probably. Poor us. His management doesn't want too many people to know he's arriving. You know how the paparazzi can get; it'd be a zoo out there."

"He'll be jet-lagged and totally intolerable. You know that, don't you?" She crossed the parking lot to the back entrance of the building. Her boss followed.

"Just don't let him get to you." Gary knew that was impossible. He'd met Kent Reynolds once and had experienced firsthand what a condescending piece of work he could be. He admired Peggy for actually accepting. He thought he wouldn't be able to talk her into it.

"Easier said than done, I'm afraid." She stopped and turned around. "I just want to hit him with something hard. Knock some sense into that self-absorbed brain of his." She continued inside, Gary followed. "He's the kind of person who knows exactly which buttons to push … and when."

"Hon, I have the utmost confidence in your professionalism." Gary didn't know how to respond to her comment about assaulting the actor. He hoped she was joking.

Peggy glared at him sideways. "Right. What if he doesn't want me to drive for him?"

"If he decides to complain he can drive himself around. But he has no option. It's a busy time of year and you're the only available driver right now."

She really wished she wasn't.

While Peggy changed into her chauffeur uniform, which consisted of a white shirt, black jeweled cravat, fitted, single breasted jacket and black tailored pants, she thought about the arrogant Mr. Reynolds. He had fallen into an acting career years ago because of his incredible good looks and steamy bedroom eyes. She had to admit he was attractive, but that was all. He had no genuine attributes or personality—none that would attract the right people into his life, anyhow. His attitude and the way he treated people was appalling. Her mind wandered back to the first night she had stayed in his hotel suite…

…The evening had started out reasonably well, until room service was late with dinner. Kent had been pacing and was clearly ticked off by the time the meal arrived. Peggy had been embarrassed when Kent berated the young room service guy for being five minutes late, even though he'd tried to explain that the hotel was a few staff down, due to the fast-spreading flu. Kent hadn't cared at all, telling him not to bother with excuses.

After the young man rushed out the door, Kent slamming it behind him, the actor turned on her, his angry eyes boring into her core. "Well," he ordered, hands on hips. "Don't just stand there looking at me like that. Sit down."

Peggy opened her mouth to respond, but he raised a dismissive hand, saying 'don't bother'.

She had really wanted to voice her opinion, but decided it would be a waste of energy. He didn't give a damn what anyone thought. Instead, she walked across, pulled out her own chair and sat down opposite him at the over-sized, circular mahogany table. Not knowing whether to attempt conversation, she ate in silence. But Kent wasn't about to let that happen.

"Peggy, isn't it?" he asked, his brooding gaze focusing on her, making her feel uncomfortable and self-conscious.

"Yes," she replied.

"Why?"

She frowned. "Why what?" she asked, her gaze meeting his. He was so good-looking, even at forty-something. Dark brown, shoulder-length hair, pale clear skin, his chin adorned by a closely cropped goatee, and beautiful, chocolate brown eyes. She couldn't understand why he chose to be so unpleasant when he had everything going for him.

"Why Peggy? Why not…?"

"Does it matter?" she countered. "Why is your name Kent? Why not Kenneth or Keith or…"

"Touché," he replied, and continued eating his meal.

Peggy studied him for a moment, trying to determine the point of their brief encounter before continuing her meal. There didn't seem to be one.

All of a sudden, Kent pushed back his chair, got up from the table, and walked across to the well-stocked bar in the corner of the large room. He took two glasses from a shelf above his head, sat them on the counter, then surveyed the bottles of wine nestled in the rack behind him. Finally sliding a bottle from its v-shaped resting place, Kent studied the label before uncapping it and pouring two glasses. He picked up the bottle in one hand, the glasses in the other and returned to the table, sitting the bottle between them.

"Here," he said, shoving the glass at her.

Peggy glanced up at him and took the wine glass from his hand, their fingers touching and sending a tingle through her body. "Thanks." She sat it on the table in front of her.

"You're not going to taste it?" Kent asked with an incredulous glare.

"Oh?" Peggy gazed at the deep red velvet liquid in the short-stemmed wine glass. "You want me to try it now?"

"You're damn right I do. That's a $500 bottle of wine. A Chateau Latour Bordeaux, to be precise." Kent moved around the table and sat down opposite her again. "So drink up, there's plenty more where that came from. And I plan to get wasted tonight." He sucked in a large mouthful of wine.

Peggy wasn't a drinker. She'd learned the hard way once at a party, when she'd consumed two glasses of wine on an empty stomach and made a complete fool of herself by climbing onto a table and doing a seductive striptease to the Marvin Gay song 'Sexual Healing' in front of her then new boyfriend, David, his mates and their girlfriends. The guys had hooped and hollered, calling 'take it off, take it off', but their girlfriends hadn't been amused, and neither had her boyfriend. Suffice to say the relationship didn't last long after that little alcohol-induced performance, and she'd promised herself never to do it again.

Kent gazed across the table, noticing she was distracted. "Where'd you go just then?"

The embarrassing memory quickly dissipated. "I beg your pardon?"

"I asked where you went. You were definitely somewhere else."

"Oh, just remembering something that happened once after a couple of glasses of wine. I'm not a big drinker."

Kent's face darkened, and he smirked at her. "Did something you regret, hm?"

She'd known exactly where his mind had gone … to sex. He'd assumed she had gotten drunk and had random sex with some guy. She decided not to elaborate and leave him wondering…

…Peggy pushed her cap onto her head, gave herself the once over in the full-length mirror, and headed out to the garage. Gary was waiting for her with the keys to the BMW 750i. She was thrilled. At last she had the chance to drive her dream car.

Her boss dropped the keys into her hand. "I know you'll take good care of this little beauty," he told her, running his hand along the glossy paintwork of the elegant, black sedan.

"Thank you." Peggy's smile broadened.

"It's the least I can do, considering."

She kissed his cheek. "You're one in a million."

Gary's face reddened. "Better get going. The king'll be arriving soon." He opened the door for her. "And you don't want to be late."

Peggy slid into the luxurious, leather seat and gave an appreciative sigh. She had died and gone to heaven—prestige car heaven that is.

The drive to the airport would take about an hour, so she could cruise along the highway, enjoy the ride, and familiarize herself with her new toy. The ride was smooth and exceptionally quiet. Peggy slid through the toll detector with the device on the dash, and continued along the Gateway freeway toward the airport.

When she drove over the crest of the Sir Leo Hielscher Bridge she could see that the traffic had ground to a halt. She slowed the limousine and stopped behind the other stationary vehicles. The freeway usually flowed smoothly and Peggy figured there must have been an accident somewhere up ahead. She turned on the radio to listen for a traffic report, and glanced at the time. Mr. Arrogant would have already landed, gone through security and, right at that moment, would be collecting his luggage. *Oh well, there's nothing I can do about that now. He'll just have to wait until I get there, won't he.*

The traffic was doing the stop-start shuffle, and as Peggy inched her way along the highway she noticed the exit sign for the airport not far up ahead, but knew it would take ages before she reached it. The female radio announcer reported that there had been a five car pileup on the north bound lanes and it would take some time to clear. Peggy sighed and drummed her fingers on the steering wheel. Kent Reynolds would be furious by the time she pulled in to collect him, and she would have to endure him berating her for not being on time all the way to the hotel.

When she got off the freeway, Airport Drive wasn't at all congested and the International Airport quickly came into view. She breathed a sigh of relief, swung the BMW around and continued up to 'Arrivals.'

Peggy pulled the limousine into the curb at the far end of the building and spotted the actor standing with an Airport Security Officer. No paparazzi in sight. They glanced over at her as the car stopped in front of them. She shrugged off the uncomfortable feeling, pressed the button on the console to pop the trunk, opened the door and stepped out of the vehicle.

"I apologize for being late, Mr. Ar … Reynolds, but there was an accident on the freeway and it held everything up." She gave him a thin smile and crossed the sidewalk to pick up his luggage.

Kent Reynolds turned to speak to the security officer, who shook his hand and walked away, then the actor approached her. "I didn't expect to see you again. I thought you'd been let go." He frowned at her, remembering their encounter in his hotel suite. After plying her with a couple of glasses of red, he'd attempted to have his way with her, until she managed to knee him in the balls. It had hurt like hell and he couldn't stand up for a good ten minutes afterward. That had been a year ago and things had changed significantly since then.

"No, Mr. Reynolds, as you can see, I'm still with the company. Our other drivers are fully booked, so you'll just have to tolerate me, I'm afraid. Now, can I take your luggage for you, sir?" She hated calling him *sir*. What she really wanted to call him was *asshole*.

Kent folded his arms across his chest. "Go right ahead." He knew she wouldn't be able to lift the large suitcase into the trunk of the limousine by herself but he thought it would be amusing to watch her try.

Peggy reached for the handle of, what appeared to be, a heavy suitcase and attempted to lift it off the ground. She couldn't. She gazed along the sidewalk, hoping there was someone who could help her, but there was no one other than the actor.

"Having some difficulty?" he asked, walking over to her. "I'd be happy to help you with it."

Peggy wasn't about to give in. If he helped her, she would have to do something for him. And she knew exactly what that would entail—sleeping with him. She swallowed the angry lump in her throat. "No thanks, I can manage." The suitcase had wheels, so she dragged the cumbersome bag across to the open trunk and struggled to get it off the curb. It was way too heavy for her to lift, she knew, but she wasn't going to give Mr. Arrogant the satisfaction of having something to use against her later.

The actor stood on the path smiling as he watched her struggle with the suitcase. He could have picked up the two flight bags and dropped them into the trunk, but he enjoyed watching her try. She was a feisty little thing committed to doing her job, no matter what.

"Are you sure I can't help you with that?" he offered.

Peggy was determined to get the suitcase into the car, one way or the other, without his help. She had no intention of becoming another of his conquests. "*No thank you*, I've got it." She knew she didn't.

"This is going to take awhile, you realize," Kent told her. "If you just let me help…'

Peggy swung around and glared at him. "You're enjoying this, aren't you? You think I'll give in and let you

18

help me, so that you can sleep with me … is that it? Do you think I've forgotten what happened last year? Well, I haven't."

Kent frowned at her. He'd been totally unaware that so many people had had such a low opinion of him. Although, he realized, he had been pretty intense back then. He'd come to understand his actions were hindering his career and his relationships, and that people didn't want to work with him or for him. In the end, he'd asked his manager for help. Eric Schwartz had offered him the name of a good therapist, and one year later Kent was a changed man. How could he explain to this woman, one he had tried to take advantage of, that he wasn't the same person she'd encountered a year ago?

"Look, I don't want anything from you. I'm only trying to help you get the bags into the car."

"Oh, right, like you do that every day."

"I've …"

Peggy raised a dismissive hand. "Don't bother. I know exactly what kind of man you are." She shivered, remembering his body pressed against hers, his tongue probing her mouth, and his roaming hands unbuttoning her blouse in his hotel suite that night.

Kent's management had offered her a meager sum in compensation, which she'd refused and had her sign a non-disclosure agreement. After that the incident was quickly swept under the carpet.

At that moment, an attractive blonde strutted out of the airport and came over to Kent. "Are we ready to go?"

"Not yet. The driver's having some difficulty getting the bags into the car." The actor pulled the young woman to him, sliding his arm around her tiny waist.

19

Peggy's mouth gaped, and she realized Kent and the nameless young woman were staring at her. The oversized suitcase had to be hers. Peggy wondered who she was. A colleague? His girlfriend? She suddenly became aware of her feelings ... was she jealous? *No, that's not possible.* She despised Kent Reynolds.

Kent moved away from the young woman. "Here, let me do that." He walked over, picked up the suitcase without effort and tossed it into the trunk. Then he picked up the other two bags, dropped them inside and closed the lid. "Can we please go now?" he asked, a look of amusement on his face.

Peggy looked into Kent's eyes, becoming lost in those amazing brown pools, and for a moment forgot where she was. She noticed that his eyes were a rich, milk chocolate color. Beautiful bedroom eyes. Her heartbeat quickened, and her face grew warm.

The young woman waiting on the path cleared her throat, snapping Peggy out of her daze. "Oh? Yes ... of course." She stepped around Kent and opened the rear passenger door.

Kent escorted the young woman over to the BMW, helped her into the vehicle, and climbed in beside her. Peggy closed the door, rushed around the car and slid into the driver's seat.

The drive to the Palazzo Versace Hotel on the Gold Coast would take some time, and as Peggy glanced into the rearview mirror and saw the pair kissing in the back seat, she realized it was going to be an extremely long drive.

Two

The condominium suite was opulent—antique Baroque décor, flat panel, plasma television encased in a beautifully crafted, wood cabinet, a modern self-contained kitchen with black marble bench tops, a well-stocked private bar, and an amazing view of the Marina. Peggy had stayed in some elegant hotel suites before, but never one as exquisite as this. It took her breath away. Kent Reynolds could afford whatever he wanted, and this was definitely five star.

The porter brought the luggage in and Kent directed him to the larger of the two bedrooms—the one with the private spa. He gave the guy a hundred dollar tip, which Peggy thought was rather generous, and thanked him.

She'd packed her non-designer, black vinyl overnight bag with a couple of changes of clothes she could mix and match, a pair of summer pajamas, a bathing suit, and her makeup case. Peggy also included a little black dress and high heels, just in case. She wandered across the elegant room to the second bedroom door, opened it and peered inside. The room was just as gorgeous, with its own bathroom. She dropped her bag onto the stool at the foot of the king-size bed, and walked over to the window. She also had a balcony and wonderful view.

A sudden knock on the door caused her to spin around. Kent was standing in the doorway. "Everything to your liking?"

Peggy gazed at her surroundings and smiled. "Yes. It's lovely."

Kent's gaze met hers and he smiled. "My pleasure," he said, turning around and walking away. Peggy rushed across to the doorway.

"Thank you," she offered.

The actor turned around and smiled again. He had an amazing smile. Perfect, in fact. Her body trembled and she hoped he didn't notice.

Peggy walked back to the window and gazed out at the glistening azure water. It was going to be an enjoyable stay. After a while, she slipped out of her jacket, tossed it onto the bed and walked out to the living room. The young woman, whom Kent had neglected to introduce at the airport, introduced herself.

"Hi, I'm Felicity." She smiled and held out her hand.

"It's nice to meet you," Peggy said, shaking it. She was more than curious. "I don't mean to pry, but are you and Kent a couple?"

Felicity giggled. "Oh, no, I'm just his companion for a few days. I work for an exclusive escort agency back in LA that caters to celebrities, politicians and high profile businessmen."

Peggy was taken aback. Why would Kent Reynolds need an escort service? He could have any woman he wanted. "You are? I don't understand. He brought you all this way for only a couple of days?"

"I'm here as a kind of hanger, you might say. When Kent attends formal dinners and other celebrity functions, he'll need an attractive arm piece." She smiled. "I'll be that arm piece this time."

"Oh, I see." Peggy studied her for a moment, frowning. "Is that all?"

Felicity glanced at her expensive, Manolo Blahnik shoes, then gazed at Peggy. "Well, no, not exactly. Mr. Reynolds is one of our best clients, so whatever he wants…"

At that moment, Kent walked out of his bedroom dressed in one of the hotel's luxurious, white cotton robes. He had showered, and his shoulder-length hair was slicked back off his face. He had also shaved off his trademark goatee. Both women gasped, more out of surprise for his new look than being overheard.

"Did I interrupt something," he asked, walking across to the bar and pouring some chilled water for himself and the ladies.

Peggy and Felicity gave each other a conspiratorial glance then looked at Kent. Peggy answered. "We were just … getting acquainted."

"Ah, so Felicity told you," he said, glancing at Peggy and giving a slight smile. He picked up the glasses of water, walked across to the ladies and handed them one each.

"Well, no. I mean…"

Kent gazed into her eyes. "No need to explain. I can see by the look on your face that she has."

Peggy didn't think she had a particular look on her face. But then, come to think of it, perhaps she did look a little shocked. Kent had brought this young woman all the way to Australia to sleep with him. Was she being a prude? Maybe. She didn't understand why he'd need to.

Felicity lowered her lashes. "I'm sorry. Wasn't I supposed to say anything?"

Kent lifted the young woman's face up to meet his gaze. "It doesn't matter." He gave her a reassuring smile and she relaxed.

Peggy watched Kent's reaction. He seemed different somehow. Kinder. Gentler. She hadn't once notice him lash out at anyone. Not the hotel staff. Not Felicity. Not even her for being late picking him up from the Airport. Had she been wrong about him?

At midnight, Kent was ready for bed. He'd been sitting in front of the over-sized television engrossed in a documentary about the universe, while Peggy and Felicity sat at the table playing card games. Dinner had been delicious—A La Carte menu and delectable, mouth-watering desserts. Kent had left the table immediately after dinner, wandering across to the television and settling in for the rest of the evening.

He stood up, stretched, turned around and gazed across at the two women sitting at the dining table. He smiled and said, "Well, I think it's time for bed. Don't you?"

Felicity got up from her chair. "Night, Peggy, it's been fun," she said, and crossed the living room to the actor.

Peggy eyes met Kent's, and her heart felt heavy in her chest. "Goodnight. See you in the morning. Oh, before you go, what time do you need the car tomorrow?" she asked, holding the actor's gaze.

"Sometime around noon, I plan to sleep in." He glanced down at Felicity and slid an arm around her waist. The pair turned and disappeared into the bedroom and the door closed behind them, leaving Peggy alone with her confused thoughts.

She sat staring at Kent's bedroom door for quite some time, the troubling scenario playing over and over in her mind. There was no way she could sleep now, knowing that he was in the next room making love to Felicity. Peggy became aware of her thoughts. "Oh, my God!" she whispered, raising a hand to her mouth. "I am jealous!" The revelation shocked her.

Kent's bedroom door opened and he stepped into the living room, only wearing a pair of body hugging, black boxers—Calvin Klein monogrammed in white around the waistband.

"Talking to yourself?" he asked, closing the bedroom door and padding barefoot across the room, past Peggy, and into the kitchen.

Seeing him dressed, or undressed that way turned her mind to putty. "Who, me?" She instantly felt stupid; who else would he be talking to?

He glanced around the room, an amused smile on his face. "I don't see anyone else here. Do you?" He poured ice water into two glasses, returned the jug to the refrigerator, walked back to Peggy and sat a glass on the table in front of her.

Peggy didn't want to look up at him—at his smooth, muscular chest and broad shoulders. At that amazing long neck that she suddenly had the inclination to lavish hot, wet kisses on. She didn't. But what choice did she have?

She had to say thank you, and to do that she had to look at him. She sighed softly and gazed up at him. "Thank you."

"You're welcome." He slid into the chair Felicity had occupied earlier. "It's almost 2.00 a.m., why are you still awake? Are you feeling all right? You look a bit flushed."

"I'm fine." She focused on the frosty glass in front of her, trying not to look at him, her mind wandering again. What was his body like under those tight-fitting boxers that grabbed his firm behind? From what she had glimpsed as he walked past, he appeared well-equipped. The warm flush spread across her cheeks.

"You don't look fine." Kent reached across and placed the back of his hand on her forehead. His touch was cool and she pulled away. He frowned at her. "You feel a bit warm to me. Do you want me to ask the hotel to arrange for a doctor to come and take a look at you?"

"No, I don't," Peggy blurted. God, he was too close. Way too close, and almost naked. She glanced at him sideways, trying to avoid looking at his gorgeous body. "Look, I appreciate your concern, but I'm not sick." She stared into his delicious, chocolate eyes. "Shouldn't you be getting back to Felicity? Won't she be wondering where you are?"

"She's asleep. There's a single fold out cot in the room. I'm on that. She doesn't know I'm gone."

Peggy's mouth gaped for the second time. "You're not … sleeping with her?"

Kent reached across and gently pushed her chin up to close her mouth. "I may be many things, but I don't need to pay for sex. Trust me on that."

Her body relaxed as though a weight had lifted off her. "So, she's just your escort to the awards tomorrow night?"

"Yes, she's just my escort." He leaned away, studying her face for a moment. "What were you thinking?"

"I wasn't thinking anything." Peggy tried to sound convincing. She moved her gaze to the glass, picked it up and took a sip of water.

Kent leaned toward her so that she couldn't avoid looking into his eyes. "You thought I'd brought Felicity out here to…"

"I'm sorry I jumped to conclusions. But with your track record what was I supposed to think?" She instantly regretted saying it.

"Touché," Kent said. "I guess I deserve that."

"What do you mean?"

He sighed and sat back against the chair. "I'm sorry about that night. I had no right doing what I did."

She gazed at her hands, fingering the frosty glass. "You were drunk."

"That's no excuse. It was a stupid thing to do. You could have made it very difficult for me, but you didn't. I appreciate that." He reached across and took her hand.

The sensation of his skin on hers sent a distinct tingle through her body. With some reluctance she slid her hand from his and stood up. "Thank you for the apology, which I accept. I'm going to bed. Goodnight." Peggy walked across to her bedroom, then turned and glanced at the actor one more time before stepping inside and closing the door.

As Kent watched her disappear into her room, something stirred inside him. He felt a pang of guilt for lying to her. Of course he'd had sex with Felicity, why wouldn't he? She was a beautiful, young woman, he was a red-blooded male, and he was paying for her time. He realized he didn't want Peggy to think he was still the same, arrogant, self-centered jerk he had been the first time they'd met, although he wasn't sure why it should matter.

Three

Peggy awoke to a beautiful, Queensland morning. She got out of bed, padded across to the sliding glass doors leading to the balcony and opened the heavy, embroidered drapes, tying them back to welcome the sunshine into her room. She stretched and relished the way her body felt. She'd had a great night's sleep. *Must be the sea air.*

She glanced at the alarm clock on the bedside table, 7.15 a.m., and wondered if anyone else was awake. She wandered across to the door, opened it and peered into the living room. All was quiet at first, but then there was movement. Peggy hoped it was Kent.

It wasn't.

"Morning," Felicity whispered, closing Kent's door quietly. She was barefoot and wearing a skimpy, short black lace negligee that hugged her body in all the right places. "Did you sleep well?"

"Really well, thanks. You?" Peggy was wearing her pyjamas; purple floral boxers and lilac singlet top. She wandered over to the kitchen. There was a selection of cereal, croissants, bagels, and two different types of seeded bread, along with an assortment of spreads sitting on the counter, and a tray with several varieties of tea and coffee. There was also a coffee maker. Peggy scooped coffee into the drip tray and started the machine. It wouldn't take long.

"Me? Oh, yeah, I slept great. Kent's an amazing stress reliever." Felicity lowered her lashes and giggled, a slight flush spreading across her cheeks.

She had a habit of giggling and Peggy assumed it must be some kind of nervous tic, but more likely immaturity. Felicity must have been around twenty two or twenty three years old. Half Kent's age, at least.

Peggy froze. Kent had lied to her. He'd told her he didn't have sex with Felicity, but now this young woman was saying he did. Or was she?

"What do you mean by he's an amazing stress reliever?"

Felicity's face flushed even more. She tip toed across the living room, stopped at the kitchen counter and whispered, "He's an *amazing* lover. He knows exactly how to please a woman, that's for sure. Oh, my God, the things he can do with his ton..."

"Please, stop!" Peggy's stomach tightened. She was so angry that he'd lied to her. He hadn't changed at all.

Felicity noticed Peggy's scowl. "Is something wrong?"

Peggy hid her feelings behind a forced smile. "What could possibly be wrong? Kent's sex life has nothing to do with me."

The young woman sighed and smiled. "Oh? Good. I thought..."

"What?" Peggy took a plate from the cupboard and sat it on the counter.

"Well, I got the feeling you had a thing for Kent. I tried to explain it to him last night before we made love, but he didn't want to listen. He just wanted to get on with it."

"Oh, Felicity, you didn't."

"I thought I could help. The way he looks at you … I was sure he had a thing for you too." She sat at the table and buried her face in her hands. "I'm sorry if I've ruined it for you. I always seem to be making dumb mistakes." Tears welled in her eyes.

Peggy felt guilty for making her feel bad. She stepped around the counter and rested a reassuring hand on Felicity's shoulder. "Don't cry. It doesn't matter now, anyway."

Felicity looked up at her, tears sliding down her face. "Thanks." She sniffled and wiped the tears away. "You know what? I'm going to pack my things and go back home."

"But what about tonight?" Peggy remembered that Kent had an awards dinner to attend.

"I'm sure he can find someone else. He's rich enough. Or maybe he can take you." Felicity padded across the room, opened Kent's door and slipped inside.

Kent emerged from his bedroom right on midday. He looked refreshed, was showered and wearing the bath robe he'd had on the previous evening. "Good morning," he said, scanning the room with a curious frown. "Where's Felicity?"

Peggy didn't want to tell him, she wasn't sure how he'd react. "She, ah, left."

"What do you mean, she left?" Kent stood with his hands on his hips, staring at her.

"Just what I said. She packed her things and said she was going to the airport."

"What? When?" Kent padded barefoot across the room and sat at the table.

"Oh, about seven thirty this morning."

"Far out." He ran a hand down the back of his head to the nape of his neck and blew out a noisy breath. "Did she say why?"

Peggy avoided answering the question. Instead, she poured coffee and brought it in to him. "Would you like a croissant or some toast or something?"

"I don't eat breakfast," he told her, picking up the mug and taking a sip. "But thanks for the coffee."

"Come to think of it, Felicity did mention something." Peggy decided to confront him about the lie.

"She did? What was that?"

"Yes. She said you were an amazing stress reliever."

Kent almost choked on his mouthful of coffee. "What?" he coughed out the word. He raised his hand to his mouth, cleared his throat, and glanced sideways at her, realising he'd been caught out.

Peggy rested her cheek against her hand and gazed up at the ceiling, as if deep in thought. "Now what was it she said? Oh, now I remember. 'He's an amazing lover. He knows exactly how to please a woman, that's for sure. Oh, my God, the things he can do with his…'"

"Stop!" Kent stared at her. "I can explain."

"I'm sure you can. Thing is, it doesn't matter." She hurried past him, into her room and locked the door.

Kent rushed across the living room and stood outside her door. "Peggy? Will you at least hear me out?" He paced. "Yes, all right, I did sleep with Felicity. I'm a guy, what did you expect? I'm sorry I lied to you. I didn't want you to think I was still the same man you met a year ago, because I'm not." He stopped pacing and listened at the door. "Peggy?"

Peggy was sitting on the balcony talking to Gary on the phone. "Please find another babysitter for Mr. Reynolds." She looked out at the glistening water. "Don't ask me what happened. It doesn't matter." Gary promised he would try and Peggy had no choice but to accept that.

She walked over to the foot of the bed, dropped the phone onto the bed cover and started packing. A quiet knock echoed into the room. "What is it, Kent?"

"I really want to set things right with you. Won't you at least open the door, so we can face each other?"

Peggy pushed her pajamas into the bag, zipped it shut, and plonked herself down onto the bed. "What can you say? You slept with Felicity and lied about it."

"Being a good guy hasn't been easy for me…"

"Oh, puhleeze," Peggy scoffed.

"Look, just listen to what I have to say, all right." He paced for a moment then stopped. "Things take time, and I am trying, but some old traits are going to stick longer than others." He paced again. "I know it sounds like a lame excuse, but think about it. You remember what I was like before. You have to admit there's been a considerable change since then. There's still some wrinkles to iron out, but for the most part, I'm a better person—a better man.

Right?" He stopped pacing and waited for the answer he hoped she would give him.

She didn't respond. She was hurt, and nothing Kent Reynolds could say would change that.

Peggy had unintentionally fallen asleep. When she woke up and saw that it was just after 4 p.m., she sat up and her sleepy gaze wandered the room. She checked her cell phone. Why hadn't Gary called back? She really needed to get out of here; she didn't want to spend another night with Kent. She slid off the bed and walked over to the door.

She eased it open and peered into the living room. Kent was nowhere to be seen. Peggy was relieved; she really didn't want a confrontation right now. She slipped out of the room and wandered across to the kitchen. Her mouth was dry from sleeping and she needed a drink. She took a glass from the cupboard and opened the refrigerator for the jug of ice water. As she closed the door, Kent was standing at the counter. She gasped and jumped backward.

"God, you scared me," she told him, holding a hand to her heart.

"I didn't mean to." His voice was tight as his serious gaze met hers. "I got a phone call from Gary Taylor a while ago."

"Oh?" Peggy looked sheepish as she poured water into the glass and returned the jug to the refrigerator.

"Yes." He studied her for a moment, frowning. "Apparently, you requested another driver to take your place. Someone named Phillip is on his way, so you're free to leave." He turned around, stalked across the living room and disappeared into his bedroom.

Peggy let out a sigh, unsure whether it was one of relief or disappointment. Had she been too hasty in her decision to leave? She thought it over. *Maybe I should call Gary back.* Phillip was a professional and would do a great job, but…

She raced across the living room and into her bedroom, leaving the door ajar. She snatched up the cordless phone and dialed.

"Hi, Gary, it's me." She sat down on the bed. "I've been thinking." Peggy bit her bottom lip. She knew how difficult it had been for Gary to find a replacement on such short notice. "Would it be okay if I stayed?"

Gary was puzzled. "But, I thought you wanted out?"

"I did. But I've had time to reconsider and…"

"Hon, what am I supposed to tell Phil? He's on his way back from vacation to do this for you." Gary rubbed a hand across his frowning brow.

"I'm sorry. He can take the next big job. It's just … I think I should stay. I don't want to leave the job unfinished. That happened the last time, remember?" She was still trying to determine her feelings for Kent, and if she left now she would never know the answer.

"He hasn't tried anything has he?"

"No, nothing like that." Peggy smiled. He was looking out for her.

Gary shook his head. "All right. I don't know what I'm going to tell Phil. Maybe he can head back to his family and finish his vacation." He sighed. "Anyway, I'll think of something."

Peggy lightened. "Thanks, Gary. You're the best."

"Whatever." He wasn't falling for her sweet-talk this time. He knew something was up. "Just be careful, okay?"

"I will, promise. Thank you. Bye." Peggy dropped the phone into its cradle and fell back across the bed, breathing a sigh she knew was one of relief. She popped up off the bed, remembering the glass of water she'd left in the kitchen. She stood up and as she pulled back the door Kent was standing there. The aftershave he had on smelt amazing, and he looked gorgeous in his dark blue, Armani pinstripe tuxedo, with a high collared, white shirt and thin, black bow tie. Her breath caught in her throat. "God!" She jumped back. "Don't do that."

Kent's frowning gaze seemed a little off to her. "I've had to arrange for another escort to join me for tonight's awards. She'll be here soon. Her name's Tiffany. I wanted to let you know so you're not *shocked* when she arrives." He turned around, walked over to the bar, poured red wine into a glass and swallowed it in one mouthful. Peggy hadn't once seen him drink the whole time they had been at the hotel, and wondered what had prompted the sudden indulgence.

She walked across to the bar.

"I figure you'll be gone by the time I get back," he said tersely, pouring more wine into the glass.

Peggy moved closer. "I've had a…"

Kent pointed to the coffee table. Peggy's gaze followed his direction. A white, business-sized envelope sat on the corner. "That's your payment. There's five thousand in it. That should cover your inconvenience."

Peggy couldn't understand his turnaround. He had suddenly reverted back to the old Kent … the man she'd despised. She frowned at him. "Why are you doing this?"

"Doing what?" He swallowed the wine and clanked the glass down on the bar. "You're leaving. I'm paying you.

It's that simple." His heart sank as he said the words, but he couldn't rescind them now. He was angry; he didn't want her to leave.

Tears welled in Peggy's eyes, but before she would give him the satisfaction of seeing her upset, she rushed into her room and slammed the door.

Kent had somehow managed to make her feel like a lady of the night being paid for services rendered.

Four

Peggy remained hidden in her room until Kent and his date left for the awards presentation. She didn't feel like facing him, or meeting the new woman he'd be sleeping with tonight. It was 6 p.m. She sat on her bed and contemplated what she would do with the few hours she had to herself. Maybe she would sneak into Kent's room and take a dip in his private spa. Afterward, she could turn on some music and dance around the living room, lip-syncing to songs by famous rock chicks like Joan Jet or Pat Benitar. Women her age still did that kind of thing sometimes—it was fun.

Her first choice sounded good to her. After dinner she would grab a fresh set of underwear and head for Kent's spa. Why not? He wasn't making use of it. She opened her bedroom door and walked into the living room. She'd called room service, so her dinner would be arriving at any minute. She had ordered Chicken Provencal, with a tossed garden salad. No dessert tonight. When room service knocked on the door Peggy rushed across to open it. She was famished.

The guy, whose tag read Warren, wheeled in the trolley and stopped inside the door. "Where would you like it?" he asked, picking up the covered plate, cutlery and napkin and waiting for her direction.

"Oh, over there's fine," Peggy pointed to the coffee table. She'd planned to eat in front of the television. "Thanks."

Warren set the plate down on the table, lifted the cloche and said, "Anything else I can get for you?" Peggy said no, and he replied, "All right, well, have a good evening." He returned to the trolley, wheeled it outside and closed the door.

Peggy opened the television cabinet and picked up the remote control. She walked back to the luxurious sofa and sat down in front of her meal. It looked delicious.

She pressed the remote and the television flashed on. The hotel supplied in house movies, and Peggy decided to see what was playing. She flicked to the movie channel, 'The Vow' was screening. She had seen it at the cinema with her friend, Janelle, and they'd loved it, laughed and cried over it. It was a bittersweet love story. She got up, walked over to the sideboard and grabbed the tissue box; a must for this movie.

By the time the movie ended, Peggy realized she would have to make it a quick dip in the spa, otherwise Kent would be back and she'd miss the chance. She picked up her plate and took it into the kitchen, then rushed to her room, grabbed her black lace underwear and a towel from her bathroom and headed to Kent's room.

Peggy opened the door, poked her head inside and gazed around the luxurious bedroom. It was amazing. She hadn't seen the room before now. She felt like a thief sneaking into his private abode. Peggy glanced at Kent's king-size bed, imagining him lying there, and found herself moving toward it. Before she could stop herself, she lay down on the beautiful Baroque cover, running her hands over its patterned surface.

The heady aroma of Kent's aftershave drifted into her nostrils, sending a shiver through her body, and Peggy moved up the bed to the European pillows. Sniffing, she found his pillow and hugged it to her, imagining how wonderful it would feel to have him in her arms. He had a gorgeous body: toned, with long athletic legs. She liked athletic legs on a man. She laid on his side of the bed, hugging his pillow for some time before realizing that if she didn't move Kent would be back with his new playmate.

Peggy snatched her underwear off the bed, smoothed the cover and headed into the bathroom. Everything was so elegant and pristine. She ran the bath, which took only minutes, turned on the massaging jets, undressed and stepped into the swirling water. She gave a contented sigh as she immersed her body in the warm foam. It felt wonderful on her skin. Lying back and closing her eyes, Peggy wondered why Kent wasn't attracted to her. He had been once. Well, he'd been drunk at the time, did that count? She looked after her body, and didn't look her forty two years. But men his age always seemed to opt for a younger model. Why? Some of them didn't have the ability to hold a decent conversation, so what was the attraction? A younger body, no doubt.

She decided not to think about him, and just enjoy the luxury around her. Before she knew it the week would over, Kent would fly back to the States, she'd go back to her mundane life, and all this would be just a memory. Peggy sighed. She didn't want it to end, and realized she had feelings for Kent—real feelings. But he had been cruel to her tonight. Was he angry with her for wanting to leave? No, that couldn't be the answer. He'd hired another woman to sleep with tonight, if he was angry or hurt by her wanting to leave he wouldn't have done that. Would he?

The swirling warm water enticed Peggy's eyes to close, and when she jolted awake she could hear voices in the other room. She blinked the haze of sleep from her eyes and sprang out of the bubbles, then glancing down at her bare breasts, sank back into the tepid water. How long had she been asleep? Kent and Tiffany were back. What was she going to do? "Oh God," she whispered. "What if he comes in here?"

Peggy made a grab for the folded towel sitting on the marble-topped end of the bathtub and it slid into the water. She gave a huffy, frustrated sigh as she snatched it out, stood up, wrapped it around her and stepped out of the spa onto the bath mat. She wouldn't be able to empty the water; it would make too much noise. There was no other way to get back to her room except through the living room. Where could she hide?

The only solution she could come up with was to turn out the light and hope Kent didn't want to entertain his playmate in the spa tonight. She would wait until they were asleep, then sneak back to her room. She flicked off the light, stepped into the dark shower cubicle, closed the opaque glass door and sat on the floor with her back against the cold tiles.

Within minutes, the bathroom light flicked on and Peggy was sure she'd been discovered. Wide-eyed, she watched the hazy figure of Kent move toward the shower door, then pass it as he headed to the toilet. She held her breath, her heart racing, and hoped he wouldn't be long. Minutes later she heard the toilet flush, and Kent crossed the room to the vanity to wash his hands. Peggy squeezed herself even further into the corner. If he saw her now, what would happen? Kent wandered back across the bathroom, stopped again at the shower door, then walked over and flicked off the light as he left. Peggy let out the breath she'd been holding, her body trembling. That had been a close call.

She could hear the pair talking and laughing in the other room. It bothered her. She wanted to be the woman Kent was talking and laughing with. God, how pathetic did that seem. He was good-looking, wealthy, and single; he could have any woman he wanted. All the same, she wished it was her.

As she sat in the dark bathroom, Peggy wondered what time it was. She knew Kent was a night owl, so she figured it would be around 1.00 a.m. or so. Peggy yawned and shivered. She was sleepy and cold. Sitting wrapped in a wet towel wasn't going to keep her warm, especially if she had to sit in the bathroom most of the night. She hoped she wouldn't have to.

The light in Kent's bedroom flashed on, and Peggy sucked in a startled breath. Tiffany was giggling … another giggler. She wondered if these women had any brains at all, or if it was just their youthful bodies that attracted Kent.

Peggy peered around the glass door and could see Kent standing at the foot of the bed. He'd taken off his tuxedo jacket and was unbuttoning his shirt. She couldn't take her eyes off him. His shirt gaped open revealing his gorgeous, hairless chest and lightly muscled abdomen.

Tiffany did a seductive strut over to Kent, clad in a red lace G string and matching strapless bra, slid his shirt off his shoulders and let it drop to the floor. She then proceeded to unclip his trousers and slide the zipper down. Peggy pushed a hand over her mouth and darted back behind the wall. The realization of the situation hit her like a sledge hammer. They were about to have sex, and she was in the next room, listening.

She heard the rustle of the bed cover, then Tiffany giggling again. Kent didn't say much in the bedroom. He hadn't said more than a few words since the couple had entered the room and got naked. Maybe he was a man of action. Peggy almost giggled when the thought popped into her head, and she pressed her hand over her mouth to stifle the sound. She came to the conclusion that he didn't sweet talk these women because they were here for only one thing—sex.

Peggy didn't want to be there, she wanted to get out. She could hear things she didn't want to hear. "Ohhh, Kent, … yes, right there. Ohhh, God, that feels … sooo good," Tiffany moaned, breathless. A sudden wave of nausea hit Peggy as it became only too obvious what Kent was doing to his playmate. She wanted to jump up and run out of the room but she was trapped, listening to Kent doing things to another woman she now wished he would do to her.

The sound of squawking seagulls woke Peggy. Her sleepy gaze wandered her surroundings and she jolted awake when she realized she was still in Kent's bathroom, and it was daylight. She pushed open the glass door, got onto hands and knees and peered around the wall. There was no movement in the bedroom. She grabbed her underwear, crawled across to the doorway and stopped. She could hear someone snoring softly. That meant they were still asleep.

Peggy breathed a sigh of relief and got up off the floor. She pressed her back to the wall and leaned forward so that she could see the bed. Both Tiffany and Kent were sleeping—him lying on his stomach on one side of the over-sized bed, and her facing away from him on the other side. Not at all like a couple who had spent the night making love.

It was time to make her escape before either one of them woke up.

Tiptoeing out of the bathroom, Peggy moved across the room, avoiding the discarded clothes lying in her path. Someone snorted and turned over. Kent. Peggy stopped and held her breath, waiting a moment before continuing. When she reached the open doorway, she hurried to her room, slipped inside and closed the door, breathing a heavy relieved sigh.

Kent would know she'd been in his spa. The tub full of cold water would make it obvious. What was she going to say? She'd cross that bridge when she came to it. Peggy remembered she wasn't supposed to be there. She smiled to herself. Perhaps he'd think Phillip used his spa, that is until he saw her. She hoped with all her heart he'd be glad she stayed.

Peggy showered and dressed. She tied her long, blonde hair into a pony tail and was much more comfortable in her clean jeans and dark purple T-shirt. She walked out of the bathroom and across to the balcony. It was a glorious Queensland day. Her moment of serenity was interrupted by a knock on the door, and Kent's voice. "Phillip? Are you awake?"

She raised a hand to her mouth and sucked in a tense breath. What would he say when he saw her? There was only one way to find out. She crossed the room and opened the door.

The actor looked genuinely shocked. "Peggy? I thought you left."

"Phillip's on leave and can't get back, so I decided to stay." She gazed into his bewildered eyes. "You don't mind, do you?"

Kent gathered his cool composure. "No, as long as there are no more dramas."

"There won't be." Peggy was taken aback by his indifference to her.

"Good." He turned around and walked across to the kitchen. Peggy followed. "That explains the spa then," he said.

"Oh, that. I just…"

"Don't worry about it," Kent dismissed. "Just don't do it again, my room is off limits." He studied her face for a moment without saying anything, then turned back to the counter and poured coffee for himself. He continued speaking without looking at her. "Tiffany and I are going out to lunch later. I'll need you to drive us to the Shogun restaurant. I hear the food's excellent." He glanced at her. "And you'll have to change. This is business."

He wanted her to wear her chauffeur's uniform. He hadn't even noticed the way she was dressed, or that she'd made up her face. She decided if it was business he wanted it was business he would get.

"Yes, Mr. Reynolds," she said. "What time?"

"We have a one o'clock reservation."

"I'll be ready." She turned and walked back to her room and shut the door, closing Kent Reynolds out of her life for a while.

Five

After dropping the actor and his date at the Shogun restaurant, and being told to pick them up around three, Peggy drove back to the hotel. She strutted to the suite, pulled off her chauffeur uniform and slipped into her maroon bathing suit. If Kent Reynolds could indulge himself, so could she. She grabbed a towel, sunscreen and her sunglasses and headed to the swimming pool.

She dropped her things onto a lounge, walked across to the edge and dived straight in, swimming the length of the pool three times to get her frustration with Kent out of her system. When Peggy surfaced, she was startled by a man standing at the edge of the pool. She gazed up at him, squinting back the glare. He was around forty-five, attractive, with dark blonde hair tied in a neat ponytail. He was tall, had a nicely toned body, was wearing a pair of Ripcurl board shorts, and standing with his hands on his hips, smiling at her. "Hi," he said.

Peggy glanced over her shoulder. There was no one else in the pool. She turned back to look at him. She gave him a curt "Hi", then swam to the end and climbed out. She walked across to the lounge, picked up the towel and wrapped it around her, then smoothed her hair to one side and squeezed out the water. The guy walked over to her.

"I'm Jeff, Jeff Birmingham," he said, his accent British. He offered his hand.

Peggy stared at his outstretched hand, then looked up at him. "Have we met before?"

He lowered his hand. "Well, no, but I hope I can change that." He had a nice smile—cheeky, in a self-assured kind of way.

"Why?" Peggy wasn't going to make it easy for this guy to hit on her.

"You look like someone I'd be interested in getting to know." He walked over to the lounge beside hers and sat down.

Peggy wasn't interested in starting something with this man, but realized he wasn't about to leave any time soon. She laid back on the lounge and slid her sunglasses on. "How would you know that just by looking at me?"

"Look, I'm here alone and would really appreciate some company … the company of an attractive woman."

"I'm working," Peggy told him.

Jeff smirked at her, an eyebrow rising above his sunglasses.

It occurred to her what he was thinking. Why did men always think with their genitals?

"I'm a *chauffeur*," she explained. "I'm here at Kent Reynolds' request."

Jeff's smirk changed to a smile. "He's staying here?"

Peggy frowned at him, realizing she shouldn't have said anything. She reluctantly answered, "Y-e-s."

"Wow." He laid back on the lounge and folded his arms across his chest. "For how long?"

"I think I've said too much already." Peggy stood up and picked up the tube of sunscreen sitting next to the lounge. "I have to go."

Jeff jumped up and blocked her way. "Would you have dinner with me?"

"I can't."

"Why not? You're only his chauffeur … right?"

"Of course I am." Peggy frowned at the presumptuous male standing in front of her.

"I apologize. That was rude of me."

"Yes, it was." Peggy tried to maneuver around him. He stepped across her path. If she moved any further she would fall into the pool. "Do you mind?" He was close to her, and she motioned for him to move out of the way.

"You haven't answered my question."

"What question?" His musky aftershave, mingled with his body scent, teased her nostrils—it was very sexy and every nerve in her body tingled.

"About dinner."

"I already told you, I'm working." Peggy's voice was tight. She was frustrated with him.

"You have to eat, don't you?" He wasn't budging.

Peggy sighed. "If I say yes will you move out of my way?"

"Absolutely." His cheeky smile widened like the Cheshire cat's.

"Ok. Satisfied?"

"Yes. Can I pick you up?" He stepped aside.

"I'll meet you. Which restaurant?"

"The Vanitas. I hear the food is world class."

"What time?" She wanted to go back to Kent's suite and get this uncomfortable encounter over with.

49

"Seven."

"Great. See you then." With that said she marched past him, disappeared into the hotel and waited for him to leave, before she headed back to the suite.

Peggy showered and changed into her chauffeur uniform. It was 2.30 p.m. She picked up her cap and wandered into the living room. Someone knocked on the door and she wondered who it could be. She crossed the room and opened the door. Jeff was standing in the hallway.

"You really are a chauffeur," he said, his appreciative gaze roaming her body.

"How did you…?" Peggy looked perplexed.

"I've made friends with a few of the staff."

"You shouldn't be here. I'm on my way out." She stepped out of the suite and closed the door.

"Picking him up, huh?"

"That's none of your business. Why are you here?" She eyed him dubiously. "Are you a journalist?"

Jeff looked sheepish.

"So that's why you asked me to dinner. To pump me for information … is that it?" Peggy pushed her cap onto her head and slid on her sunglasses.

"As a matter of fact no."

"No, you're not a journalist, or no you don't plan to pump me for information?"

Jeff sighed. "Yes, I'm a journalist, but no, I wasn't planning to get information from you about Mr. Reynolds. I'd like to have dinner with you. Nothing more."

Peggy frowned at him. "In that case dinner's off." She stepped around him and marched briskly along the hall.

Jeff turned around. "I would really like to get to know you. At least tell me your name."

When Peggy reached the Shogun restaurant Kent was escorted out to the street alone. She pulled into the curb and he climbed into the front passenger seat. Peggy glanced past him, wondering where his companion was.

Kent followed her gaze, then turned to look at her. "Tiffany's gone."

"Oh?" Peggy flipped the indicator on and waited to ease the BMW into the stream of traffic. "What about her things?"

"They were collected."

"Do you want to go back to the hotel?" she asked, merging the limousine into a gap in the traffic.

"Yes, thanks."

The drive was quiet until Kent spoke. "What did you get up to today?"

"Me?" Peggy glanced at him sideways then returned her gaze back to the road. "I went for a swim in the hotel pool and met a British guest. He asked me to dinner."

Kent's expression darkened. "Did you accept?"

"Yes. Why shouldn't I? I'm not attached, and he's rather attractive. Forty-something, tall, shoulder-length blonde hair, a nice body. We met by the pool that's how I know." She felt good about telling him. He deserved it. She wasn't about to let him know she'd cancelled the dinner plans, though.

"I see. Well, have a good time." He folded his arms across his chest and gazed out the passenger window.

"Oh, I plan to."

Kent didn't speak the rest of the drive back to the hotel, and once out of the car headed straight to the suite.

Peggy decided to give him some time to brood. She knew he would.

When she entered the hotel lobby, Jeff appeared out of nowhere. "Hi, Peggy."

She glanced at him sideways, realizing one of his hotel contacts must have given him her name. "I thought I made it clear earlier," she said, continuing through the lobby.

"I was hoping you'd change your mind." He stepped up beside her. "I'm a nice guy once you get to know me."

Peggy stopped and looked at him. "All right, Mr. Nice Guy, now that you know where I'm staying you can pick me up."

Jeff looked surprised. "You're saying yes?"

"I'll see you at seven." She kept moving.

Peggy was going to make Kent so jealous that he would want to be with her. She wanted Kent Reynolds and she was going to do everything she could to get him.

Peggy stood in front of the full-length mirror, turning left and then right to check the line of the little black dress she hadn't worn before tonight. As she ran her hands down the smooth fabric, she realized she looked good—very good.

She had styled her hair long and straight, put faux diamond studs in her ears, applied just enough makeup to look elegant, and sprayed her body with *J'adore* perfume, a gift from her sister. She padded around the bed and stepped into her strappy, black high heels to finish the outfit, then took one last look in the mirror before walking into the living room. Peggy knew Kent would be waiting to see what she was wearing tonight. Her stomach tightened with anticipation as she stepped through the doorway.

Kent was lying on the sofa reading a novel. He was dressed casually—gray, knee-length, loose-fitting board shorts and a body hugging, white, DKNY sleeveless T-shirt. When he saw her, he sat up and discreetly ran his gaze over her from head to toe.

It was 6.50 p.m. Jeff would be arriving soon, so there was just enough time for the first act to play out.

"What do you think?" she asked, closing her door, walking over to him and doing a complete 360 degree turn.

Kent studied her again. The look on his face said everything. He was jealous. "You look … nice," he offered, although inside his body was screaming to take her in his arms and kiss her, hard. She looked incredible.

Peggy met his gaze and smiled, more from satisfaction than anything else. "Thanks," she said. "I appreciate the masculine evaluation before my date arrives."

Kent got up, walked across to the bar and plucked a wine glass from the shelf. He uncapped a new bottle of red and poured a glass for himself. "Peggy?"

"Yes?" She walked seductively over to the bar.

Kent gazed into her eyes and frowned, but said nothing.

"Yes, Kent?" Peggy prompted.

"Never mind." He shook his head and sucked in a large mouthful of wine. At that moment, a knock echoed into the room and Kent turned his brooding gaze toward the offending noise. "Well," he said, "your date's early."

"Yes, he is," Peggy said, not letting on that she was irritated by the interruption. She wanted to hear what Kent had to say. She crossed the room and opened the door.

Jeff looked very handsome. His hair was tied back and his face clean shaven. He wore a black sports jacket, blue button through shirt, open at the neck, and blue jeans. Peggy recognized the same aftershave she had smelt by the pool. He leaned in and kissed her cheek, then passed her a single white rose. "You look amazing," he said.

Peggy could feel Kent's jealous gaze boring into her back. "Thank you," she said, taking the rose. She reached for Jeff's hand, tugged him playfully into the room and closed the door. "I'll just put this in water. Have a seat, I'll be right back."

Jeff walked across the room to the sofa, and as he passed the bar he greeted the actor. "Hello, Mr. Reynolds, it's good to meet you." He sat down.

Peggy watched Kent from the kitchen. He did not look at all happy. She was more than pleased. Her plan was working.

"Thanks," he said, eyeing the guy darkly. "And you are?"

Peggy rushed back into the room. "I'm so sorry, where are my manners? Kent this is Jeff Birmingham. Jeff, Kent Reynolds." She motioned toward the bar.

Jeff stood up beside Peggy, sliding his arm around her back. "Are you ready to go?"

She looked at him and smiled. "Yes, I am."

"Great. Let's go." Jeff led her over to the door, then turned around to look at the actor. "Don't worry, I'll have her back in plenty of time for work." Peggy stepped out of the room and he followed her, closing the door behind them.

Six

Kent paced the living room. It was 1.30 a.m., and no sign of Peggy. Where the hell was she? Oh, he knew exactly where she was. With Jeff … in his room … in his bed. He ran his fingers through his hair and gave a heavy sigh, trying to dislodge the disturbing image from his mind. Why hadn't he told her how he felt about her? Why was he being such an ass? He continued to pace and berate himself. Finally, he realized if he didn't stop he'd drive himself insane. He walked over to the bar and picked up the wine bottle. It was empty. God, he was drinking again and she was the reason. He glanced at the clock, almost 1.45 a.m.

Disgusted with himself, he tossed the bottle into the bin and walked over to his bedroom door. Just as he reached it he heard the electronic lock click back and he ducked into his room, pushed the door to, leaving it ajar.

Peggy stepped into the living room, shoes in hand, and checked for Kent. He must have gone to bed. She was disappointed. She'd hoped he would be awake and concerned about her whereabouts, wondering if she was having amazing sex with Jeff. Not that she would on a first date, but Kent didn't know that.

The evening had been wonderful. Jeff, as it turned out, was a nice guy, just as he'd claimed. He was intelligent, witty, and well-read, among other things. As a journalist, he had been to some amazing places and met some incredible people. He was also a single parent with two grown sons. They'd had a great conversation over dinner, which he paid for, and she had enjoyed being with him. And, he was a perfect gentleman, pulling out her chair and helping her into her seat, and out again at the end of the evening.

She felt guilty for using Jeff as a pawn in her game, but if she was going to accomplish her task of making Kent Reynolds fall in love with her she needed him. He asked to see her again and she accepted. They were going out of the hotel for lunch tomorrow, and as Kent had no prior engagements, she knew it wouldn't be a problem. She would tell him in the morning.

As she padded across the living room, Kent emerged from his bedroom wearing another pair of body-hugging, Calvin Klein boxers. White ones, this time. "Oh, are you just getting in?" he asked casually, walking across to the kitchen.

"Sorry, did I wake you?" Peggy was pleased he'd gotten up. He would notice the time and wonder where she had been.

"No, you didn't wake me. I was thirsty." He poured a glass of water, returned the jug to the refrigerator, picked up the glass and walked back to his bedroom door. He lingered in the doorway. "How was your evening?" he said.

"Jeff's a really nice man. We had a great time." Peggy tried not to stare at Kent's body, but it was difficult. The clinging white boxers were almost transparent, and her body was reacting to them. Her stomach tightened and her body trembled. "Well, I'd better get some sleep. Goodnight." She rushed across to her room, slipped inside, closed the door and leaned against it—her heart racing and the moist spot between her thighs throbbing.

Seven

Peggy was eating breakfast and reading the morning newspaper when Kent emerged from his room. It was early for him, and Peggy wondered if he had something important on his agenda that he'd neglected to mention. He padded across the living room, in nothing more than the white boxers, and sat opposite her. Peggy almost choked on her coffee as he watched her from across the table.

"That was an odd time to be getting in last night," he said, leaning back against the chair and keeping his scrutinizing gaze on her.

Peggy shrugged. "Really? I didn't know there was any set time limit for a date." She put her cup down on its saucer and turned the page—a good excuse not to have to look at him.

Kent sighed. "Did you go back to his room?"

Peggy looked up from the paper, scowling. "That's none of your business. Do I ask you who you've slept with … or when?"

"You know who I've slept with." He folded his arms across his bare chest.

"Only because you make it so blatantly obvious," she told him, her voice tight.

"At least I'm honest about it," he countered, leaning forward and resting his elbow on the table. "Was he good?"

The muscles in his chest and shoulders rippled, sending a distinct message to Peggy's womanhood. She shifted her gaze to the newspaper. "Like I said, it's none of your business."

Kent was furious. His dark gaze remained on her for some time before he got up from the table, stalked back to his room and slammed the door.

A smile of satisfaction spread across Peggy's face. He was absolutely livid. She wondered if she should squeeze more lemon juice into the cut. She hated doing it, but yes she should. She got up from the table, walked across to his door and knocked.

"Kent? I meant to tell you … I have a lunch date with Jeff today." She waited, knowing he would open the door at any second. She counted down in her head: five, four, three, two, one. The door swung open to reveal Kent standing in the doorway with a white towel wrapped precariously around him.

Peggy's mouth went dry. Why did he have to look so sexy?

"You what?" he asked, holding the towel together at his waist. One long, athletic leg appeared through the gap, and it took all of Peggy's strength not to reach out and touch him. Her pulse quickened.

"I…" She licked her lips. "I have a lunch date…"

"With Mr. Fabulous?"

"That's what I said, isn't it?" She regained her composure and glowered at him, folding her arms across her chest. "I wanted to let you know in case you had anything happening that you forgot to mention."

Kent's serious expression darkened. "No, I don't have anything on my agenda for today." He tried to tuck in the towel, but it came apart. He grabbed for it as it slipped from his body and held it across his groin.

Peggy gasped and darted back. There was way too much skin. She took another step backward. "I … I have to go." She rushed to her door.

"Peggy, wait." Kent followed her, pulling the towel around him and tucking it in. "Look, I'm sorry for giving you the third degree before, it's just, I don't want to see you get hurt." He touched her arm.

She gasped, and he turned her around to face him, both hands on her arms now.

"Every time I touch you, you freeze up or pull away," he said. "Am I that repulsive to you? You said you accepted my apology for what happened last year, but it looks to me like you haven't."

Peggy frowned. "I have," she told him, hoping he couldn't see her true feelings. Not now.

He shook his head. "I don't think so." He stepped closer and stared into her eyes.

"I have forgiven you," she said, breathless. "Please let me go."

"Why can't you bear for me to touch you?" He didn't remove his hands.

"I can. It's just. It would be the same if any man touched me," she lied. Her reaction was purely him.

"Like Jeff?" The green-eyed monster reared its ugly head again.

"We haven't." She shook her head. God, he was melting through her resolve, standing there in a towel that threatened to give way at any moment and leave him naked in front of her.

"Then, where were you all that time?" His hands traveled up her arms to her shoulders, the sensual sensation of skin on skin sending a wave of electricity through Peggy's body.

"Talking." She shivered, knowing he could feel it. "Just talking."

Kent ran one hand along her shoulder to her throat, propped his thumb under her chin and raised her face up to meet his gaze. She gave him a furtive glance, her breathing shallow. He stepped closer and pulled her face to him, their lips almost touching, and when he spoke she could feel his breath on her mouth. "I'm glad that's all you were doing," he whispered, holding her gaze for a moment longer, before removing his hand, turning around and walking back to his room.

Peggy remained pinned to the spot, her body pulsing with desire. Kent had wanted to kiss her, she'd felt it. She ached for him to kiss her. Why didn't he? Peggy pulled her dazed senses back to reality, slipped into her room and closed the door. He was still attracted to her.

Lunch with Jeff had been very entertaining. He'd organized a picnic basket and driven her into the Gold Coast Hinterland. They had spent a lovely relaxing day, eating, drinking a nice chardonnay, and talking. She'd come to realize that he wasn't what she originally thought him to be, some kind of womanizer. He was a very decent man. She felt totally comfortable alone with him in that beautiful, secluded place, and when he kissed her cheek outside the suite, she hadn't minded at all. He promised to call her, saying he hoped they could get together again before she left.

When Peggy entered the suite, she could hear a woman's voice echoing out of Kent's bedroom. She stopped. Did he have someone with him, or could it be the television? She slipped out of her shoes and crept over to his door. She leaned in, straining to hear through the elegant, solid wood panel. She bit her lip and held her breath.

The door swung open and the young woman almost walked into her. Peggy stiffened and glanced at Kent, who was right behind the blonde. She looked at Peggy flustered, blushed and said, "Oh? Hi." Then she turned, kissed Kent on the cheek and said, "Thanks for the acting lesson, Mr. Reynolds. I'm sure it will help me with the audition next week." She hurried across the room and out the door.

Peggy looked at Kent in disbelief. The blonde had been wearing a hotel name tag, and she wondered if he had any scruples at all.

Kent smirked at her. "How was your lunch date with Mr. Wonderful?" He brushed past her and wandered over to the bar.

"It was very nice. Jeff treats me like a lady."

"Whoop de fricken do," Kent exclaimed, pouring a brandy. He gulped it down in one mouthful. "I guess you're wondering about blondie?" He pointed at the closed door, the empty glass still in his hand.

"It's none of my business." Peggy walked across to her bedroom.

"I saw the look you gave me—the disapproving look." He poured another brandy.

Peggy turned around. "I was surprised, sure, but I don't think I gave you a look."

Kent wagged an accusatory finger at her. He was drunk. He'd probably been drinking for the better part of the day. "Oh, yes you did." He came toward her. "You are so self-righteous, Miss … Miss … what the hell's your last name?"

She stepped backward. "Maybe you should go and sleep it off. We can talk about this later."

"Don't avoid the question. Tell me." He stopped only inches from her.

Peggy sighed. "My last name is Anton. Happy now?" She folded her arms across her chest.

"Yes, Miss Anton, I am." He pointed at her. "You shouldn't judge people it's not nice."

"I don't judge people." She was insulted by his inaccurate perception of her.

"Oh, yes you do," he declared. "I saw the look in your eyes. You looked at me like I was some kind of deviant or predator."

"I was surprised. That's all." Peggy took another step backward.

Kent moved closer, his thoughts shifting to the British guest. "Are you going to see Mr. Wonderful again?"

"I might. He's a nice man." She slid her hand along the door of her room, reaching for the handle.

"Of course he is." Kent paced, then stopped and glared at her. "Have you ever thought he's being nice to get you into bed? Men do that, you know. I've done it for chrissakes."

Peggy stepped back and turned the handle on her door. "He's not like that."

"Sure he is, if he's a normal, red-blooded male."

"You really should go and lie down. You … you don't look good."

Kent jerked himself toward her, his eyes menacing. "Why? Afraid?"

She nodded, her eyes wide. "I haven't seen you like this since that night."

He pulled back, realizing she was right. He hadn't reacted in this way since he tried to sleep with her. He frowned. "I'm sorry," he said, then turned on his heel and disappeared into his room.

Eight

Tomorrow would be her last day with Kent. The week had flown by so fast. If he didn't let her know how he felt about her, they would part and never see each other again. Peggy didn't want that to happen, but she also didn't understand what had happened to him. He seemed so different to how he was at the beginning of the week, more like the old Kent Reynolds.

As she lay in bed pondering how she would say goodbye to Kent, she heard an usual sound coming from the other room. She sprang up and listened, then threw back the covers, got out of bed and opened the door just enough to peek out. She gazed around the living room, but couldn't see anything that could make the noise she'd heard.

Peggy swung the door back, scanned the room again, and that's when she noticed Kent in the kitchen making breakfast. He gazed across the room at her.

"Good morning," he said, flipping a pancake over in the pan. He didn't miss a beat.

Peggy frowned and crossed the living room. "What are you doing?"

"What does it look like?" He slid the pancake onto a plate and poured more mixture into the pan. "I'm making breakfast." He eyed her up and down and smiled. "Cute pajamas, by the way."

Peggy had forgotten she was wearing her short pajamas, and felt her face grow warm. She backed up. "I'll just go get dressed and…"

Kent came into the dining room and set a plate down on the table for her. "Don't bother, they're ready." He walked back into the kitchen.

She felt self-conscious standing there in boxer shorts and a singlet top that accentuated her bare breasts beneath it. Her nipples hardened at the thought of him looking at her, and Peggy folded her arms across her chest. "I really should go put some clothes on."

"And let breakfast get cold? You look fine to me, more than fine. Come sit down and eat." He picked up his plate, walked into the room and sat at the table. He was wearing the hotel robe, which she was grateful for.

With some reluctance, Peggy padded over to the table and sat down, hunching forward so that Kent wouldn't notice her erect nipples through her thin top. She wondered what had caused his sudden turnaround.

Kent passed her the maple syrup and butter. "You can't eat pancakes without these."

"Thanks," she said, smiling. The situation felt rather surreal to her.

"I was wondering, as tomorrow's our last day together, could I take you to lunch? To make up for the way I've behaved. I know I've been a total pain in the ass." He gave her that dazzling smile, and she felt butterflies flitting about in her stomach.

66

"Lunch would be lovely. Thank you." She dropped a curl of butter onto the stack of pancakes, then poured maple syrup over them. They smelt so good. "Where did you learn to make pancakes like these?" she asked, not wanting to admit he had been a total jerk.

"My mom. She's a great cook. When I was a kid, she used to throw some amazing dinner parties."

Peggy breathed in the buttery aroma, then cut into the stack, lifted a fork-full to her mouth and popped it in. She sighed. They were delicious.

Kent watched her, smiling. "Good?"

She chewed quickly, not wanting to answer with a mouthful of food, and swallowed. "Very good."

"I'm glad you like them." Kent picked up his cutlery and cut his stack, which was already soaked in butter and syrup. He heaped some onto his fork and pushed it into his mouth. He gazed across the table. She was very attractive and extremely cute in her pajamas, trying to conceal her breasts from him. "Where would you like to go for lunch?" He put down his knife and fork, wiped his mouth on the serviette and stood up. "Coffee?" he asked, walking into the kitchen.

Peggy raised a hand to her full mouth. "Yes, thanks." She thought about his question. "Maybe we could eat here at the Vanitas restaurant. Would that be all right?"

Kent picked up the mugs and came back into the dining room. "Anywhere you want to go is fine with me."

She couldn't believe Kent's complete change of attitude. Had he admitted to himself that he cared for her, that tomorrow was their last day together and they may never see each other again? She hoped so.

He sat a mug in front of her and took his seat. "You're

sure you don't want to go somewhere else? You must know some great places to eat around here."

Peggy wiped her mouth on her serviette. "Yes, I do, but…"

"You'd still prefer to eat here?" He gave her a curious frown.

She didn't want to tell him that she'd prefer to spend as much time as she could with him, and not have to drive him around. She was going to miss him so much. "The Vanitas is a lovely restaurant."

"All right. I'll make a reservation for 12.30. Is that good for you?"

"Yes." Peggy gazed across the table at him, she was having difficulty adjusting to the Kent she had met at the beginning of the week.

Kent noticed her expression. "What is it?"

Peggy glanced at her plate. "I'm not sure how to put this, but…"

"Ah, I get it. You're wondering why I'm being so nice."

"Well, yes, we've had a difficult few days and…"

"What better way for me to make it up to you." He smiled at her, reached across the table and rested his hand on hers.

She loved the feel of his skin on hers. But what she wanted more than anything was for him to kiss her.

Kent slid his hand from hers and stood up. He looked down at her for a moment, then leaned in and kissed her. It lasted only a few seconds, but it was still a kiss.

Peggy was stunned. She sat in a daze, savoring the feeling, and when she opened her eyes Kent was gone. She looked around the room and in the kitchen. Where had he disappeared to so quickly? She stood up, noticing his bedroom door was open and wandered over to it. When she reached it she could hear the shower running.

Unable to stop herself, Peggy stepped through the doorway and moved toward the bathroom on trembling legs. Kent was standing inside the steamy glass cubicle. His muscular back and firm behind caused her heart to flutter. She stood mesmerized by his gorgeous wet body and wanted to strip down and slip underneath the spray of hot water with him. Touch him. Taste him. Tease him. Realizing she shouldn't be there watching him she turned to leave.

"Why don't you join me?" Kent turned around; strings of soapy bubbles sliding down his smooth chest and abdomen and pooling at his groin.

Peggy froze. Her breath caught in her throat making it difficult to breathe. She swallowed hard and turned around.

Kent stepped out of the shower and came toward her.

Peggy's heart was beating so fast it felt like butterfly wings flitting against her ribs. Her eyes widened. Her breathing quickened.

Kent pulled her to him, and covered her mouth with his—his soft, warm lips seductively gentle at first, teasing her, then firmer as the pent-up heat rose between them.

Peggy responded by wrapping her arms around him.

Kent roamed his hands down her body and tugged at the hem of her singlet top. He peeled it off over her head, dropped it to the floor, and moved his mouth to one firm breast, sucking the nipple and flicking it with his tongue.

Peggy moaned, grabbing his wet, shoulder-length hair between her fingers.

Kent pushed her against the tiled wall and trailed hot moist kisses up her slender neck, then pressed his hungry mouth to hers again, sliding his tongue between her lips and massaging her tongue.

Peggy pulled her mouth free, breathless, and stared into his eyes. They were dark with lust. She could feel his arousal pressing against her stomach and wanted to reach down and touch him, but didn't dare.

As if Kent could read her thoughts, he grabbed her hand and moved it toward his pulsing length. "Touch me," he whispered, his voice husky.

She wrapped trembling fingers around his hard flesh, moving rhythmically, and Kent growled. It was wonderful having his naked body pressed against hers, and now she knew what had been hidden beneath those body-hugging boxers.

Pleasing him heightened her senses, and she ached for him to touch her too.

Kent massaged her breasts, squeezing the nipples gently between his thumb and finger, while lavishing slow kisses up her throat and pressing his mouth to hers. Again, as if he could read her thoughts, he roamed one hand down the smooth skin of her stomach, inside her satin boxers, and slid his finger into her warm wetness, connecting with the super-sensitive nub.

Peggy moaned, breathless. Kent knew exactly how to pleasure a woman, his skilled fingers deliciously teasing the slick, tender spot, circling and squeezing to heighten the intense sensation.

Kent's arousal was driving him crazy. He wanted her, wanted to slide inside her, wanted to feel the moist, soft folds of her sex envelop his rock hard flesh. He pulled his mouth from hers and trailed hot, urgent kisses down her stomach to where his hand had been tantalizing her senses. He knelt at her feet, tugged her boxers to her ankles and pushed his mouth between her thighs, sliding his silky tongue around the taut, throbbing nub.

Every nerve ending in Peggy's body exploded in a pleasurable rush and she could no longer hold the words inside. She moaned out a husky, "Yes, Kent, yes."

He rose to his feet, swept her into his arms and carried her to the bedroom. Peggy sighed blissfully as he eased her onto his unmade bed, climbed over her and remained on hands and knees, gazing into her eyes.

Peggy pulled him to her. "Make love to me."

Kent lowered his slick naked body onto hers…

…The continuous beep of the bedside clock woke Peggy with a start. She sprang up in bed, hit the snooze button and gazed around the room, realizing it had all been a dream. A vision of her unfulfilled fantasy. Feeling bitterly disappointed, she burst into tears and threw herself against her pillows. She wanted nights like that with Kent, wanted to do those things to him. Wanted to love him and be loved by him.

Her distressed thoughts were interrupted by a knock on the door.

It opened and Kent peered around. "Are you all right? Why are you crying? I heard you moaning, aren't you feeling well?"

Peggy sniffed back the tears and wiped her eyes on the sheet. She didn't turn over to face him. "Please go away." How embarrassing, he'd heard her moaning in her sleep.

Thank God she hadn't called out his name—at least she hoped she didn't.

Kent pushed the door open, walked across to the bed and sat down. "Something's obviously upset you, and I'm not leaving until you tell me what it is."

"I don't want to talk about it." She held in another sob, having him so close only made her body ache for him even more.

"I'm not leaving." He folded his arms across his chest.

Peggy sighed and turned over. "It was just a stupid dream."

He frowned at her, concerned. "Look at me."

"Why?" She kept her gaze on her bed cover.

"Because I asked you to." He leaned in to her.

She turned away from him.

"What aren't you telling me?"

"There's nothing to tell."

"You were moaning…" At that moment it occurred to him the kind of dream she'd been having. "Were you having sex in your dream? Is that what upset you?"

Peggy still wouldn't look at him. "If I'd been dreaming about having sex, why would that upset me?"

"Don't do that."

"Do what?"

"Answer with a question." He grabbed her chin gently and turned her face toward him. "I want to help you."

"Well you can't. This conversation is over. I need to take a shower." Peggy moved his hand away, slid out of bed and pulled the door open. "Thanks for your concern, but I'm fine. Really." She motioned for him to get up.

Kent stood up and pushed his hands into the pockets of his robe. "Not so fast. I came in here to comfort you, and now you're fobbing me off? I don't think so. You owe me an explanation."

Peggy glared at him. "My dreams are my business. I don't owe you anything."

"Was I in your dream? Is that the reason you won't tell me?"

Peggy was stunned. How could he come to that conclusion? It could have been Jeff, for all he knew. She didn't want to answer his question, but she knew he wouldn't let it go. She sighed. "All right. Yes. Now will you leave?"

"Why were you crying?" She didn't answer. "Was it because when you woke up and realized it was a dream you were disappointed?"

Peggy frowned into his face. "How can you know...?"

"Because I've felt the same way." He gave a thin smile.

"What?"

He took her hand in his. "I've dreamt about us, and when I woke up I couldn't believe how real it had been."

Heat spread across her cheeks.

Kent smiled. "You're blushing, you know." He reached across and tucked stray strands of hair behind her ear.

Peggy loved him touching her. She covered his hand with hers.

"We could change all this." Kent leaned in to her. "We could make our dreams a reality"

"How?" Peggy's stomach tightened. She knew what he was about to suggest.

"We could spend the day making love." Kent kissed her lips gently and brushed her cheek with his fingertips.

It wasn't at all the way Peggy had imagined. She moved away from him. "If you want a relationship with me it has to be a *real* one. I want romance, candlelit dinners, movies. I don't want just one day in bed with you."

Kent frowned at her. "I'm leaving for the States tomorrow. How do you expect me to do what you're asking?"

"Yes, I know. That's why I can't do this." She slid her hand from his. "I'm not just a one night stand, Kent."

"That's not what I'm saying."

"Are you telling me you're ready for a fully committed relationship?"

"Not exactly, but…"

Peggy stood up. "That's what I thought. You should go now. I'd really like to take that shower."

Kent stood up and stared into her eyes. He had feelings for her, and it could be love, but he wasn't ready to be tied down. He didn't try to argue with her, he turned and walked out of the room.

Peggy shut the door, leaned against it, closed her eyes and sighed. She was still disappointed. Disappointed with the dream, disappointed with Kent's attitude, and disappointed with herself for not taking him up on his offer.

Nine

The drive to the Brisbane International Airport was silent. Kent sat in the back seat, gazing out of the passenger window. Peggy wanted to tell him she was going to miss him, and perhaps on his next visit they could get together for drinks or dinner. Maybe she could drive for him again, spend time with him. She glanced into the rearview mirror and met Kent's brooding gaze. She averted her eyes back to the road and decided it would be better not to say anything. He probably didn't want to hear it, anyway.

When Peggy pulled the limousine into the curb outside the Departures terminal, Kent flung the passenger door open and got out. She wondered if he was angry with her for not sleeping with him. She hoped that wasn't the reason for his dark mood. She popped the trunk and got out of the BMW. Kent walked to the rear of the limousine, pulled his bags out of the trunk, sat them on the sidewalk and slammed the lid shut. He definitely had something on his mind.

She walked over to him. "Is something wrong?"

"What could possibly be wrong?" he asked, folding his

arms across his chest. "I'll be leaving for the States in an hour, and you'll go back to your life."

Peggy touched his arm. "I'll miss you." She hadn't meant to say it, but there it was—the truth of her feelings finally out in the open.

Kent frowned at her. "I've been a pain in the ass, why would you miss me?"

She rubbed his arm. "Because I will." Tears stung her eyes and she blinked them back. She tried to smile. "And you haven't been a *total* pain in the ass."

"I'm sorry for everything. I wish things could have been different between us." He wanted to kiss her, but didn't dare in case a photographer was lurking somewhere nearby.

"I know. Me too." She gave a thin smile. "Well, have a safe flight. You have my number. Maybe I'll hear from you some time." She turned around to go back to the car.

Kent grabbed her arm. "Wait. I want to tell you something."

Peggy looked at him. "What is it?"

"I do care for you, Peg. Maybe, some time in the future, we can…"

"It's all right, Kent, you don't have to say that."

"Yes, I do. I'm just not ready to settle down right now. That doesn't mean I won't be at some point."

"I appreciate that, really I do, but I'll be fine. Honestly." Peggy leaned up and kissed his cheek, then turned and walked around to the driver's door and opened it. "I really hope I see you again. I *will* miss you." She smiled at him then got into the limousine and drove away, leaving Kent standing on the curb watching her go.

Kent sat in the First Class departure lounge, knowing he would miss Peggy. He'd let her get under his skin, and despite the other women, he now realized just how much she had come to mean to him. When he suggested they spend the day making love, he'd meant it. Not in the way Peggy had thought, he wanted to be close to her. Men were different to women—well that was obvious—mainly in the way they expressed their feelings. Women were emotional, whereas men were corporeal, demonstrating how they felt by the physical contact. He had really wanted to do that with her. Wanted to *show* her how much she meant to him.

He wondered how Peggy was feeling. Was she upset that he was leaving? He hoped so, because he felt like hell. He wanted to see her again, and would the next time he was in the country. Kent reached into the pocket of his jeans and pulled out the note paper she had given him. He unfolded it and looked at the writing. She had nice handwriting. *Should I give her a call before takeoff?* He decided to give it a try. He keyed the number into his cell phone and waited. The phone rang for quite a while and then her voicemail kicked in. Kent didn't leave a message.

Peggy didn't answer her phone. She knew it was Kent. She couldn't talk to him. After leaving the airport, she had pulled off Airport Drive, parked and cried her eyes out. If she answered the phone, he'd hear the thickness in her voice, and she didn't want him to feel bad during his flight home.

She sniffed back the tears, slid her sunglasses over her puffy eyes, gathered her composure, started the engine and headed for the on ramp to the Gateway freeway. Gary would be wondering where she was, soon enough, and would call her. Peggy didn't feel like explaining. She cruised through the toll detector and continued along the freeway, heading to the coast.

It would be a long, lonely drive back to her old life. Peggy glanced into the rearview mirror and Kent's image appeared, gazing back at her. She wondered how long it would be before he came out to Australia again, and whether they would still feel the same way about each other by then. She knew her feelings wouldn't change, but Kent was an entirely different matter.

As she eased the BMW into the limousine company's garage, Peggy gave a heavy sigh. It had been a long and difficult week and she knew, once again, it would take time to get over Kent Reynolds. Because, this time, she knew she was in love with him. Maybe she should have told him. No. He'd made it clear he wasn't ready to commit to a relationship. What good would it have done baring her soul to him?

Peggy opened the door and as she got out of the car, Gary emerged from the office. "How'd it go?" he asked, a concerned expression on his face.

"It went well. I'm sorry I called and caused problems for you. I guess I overreacted." Peggy gave him a thin smile and dropped the limousine keys into his hand. She leaned across, picked up her overnight bag from the passenger seat and closed the door.

"So, what happened between you two? What made you want to come home?" He glanced at the keys in his hand, then looked at her.

"It was a misunderstanding, that's all. We worked it out and everything was fine," Peggy lied. Things hadn't really been worked out at all. She had no idea where she stood with Kent or whether she'd ever see him again.

"That's good to hear."

Peggy passed her boss and headed for her car parked in the far corner of the garage. He followed her.

"I'll be glad to get home, take a hot shower and get some sleep." She unlocked the door, threw her bag onto the passenger seat and got in. "Call me when you need me."

"I will."

Peggy started the engine and said goodbye. She backed out of the garage and was looking forward to getting home. She needed some time alone to sort out her feelings.

Ten

The musical tone of Peggy's telephone continued its incessant jingle as she padded out to the living room in her dressing gown, towel drying her hair. She wrapped her damp hair in the towel, rushed across to the coffee table and snatched up the phone, hoping it was Kent. It had been two weeks since he'd flown out of Australia, and not one word. She pushed the button and pressed the phone to her ear.

"Hello?" Her voice was anxious.

"Peggy?"

"Who's this?" She frowned.

"You've forgotten me already? Oh, that is sad. I thought I'd made a better impression than that," the British male voice said.

Peggy crossed her living room and closed the drapes. "Jeff?"

"Good job," he said. "Give the lady a kewpie doll."

"How did you get my number?" Peggy sat down in the armchair next to the window.

"Ah, I hate to tell you this, love, but you're in the phone book," Jeff told her, amusement in his voice.

"I know that," Peggy snapped. She bit her bottom lip and winced at her brisk tone. "I'm sorry. It's … a surprise to hear from you, that's all."

"A pleasant one, I hope?"

Peggy knew how she must have sounded, as though his call was an inconvenience. "Yes, of course," she lied. She'd been hoping it was Kent and did feel Jeff's call was an intrusion.

"The reason I'm calling is I was hoping we could get together for dinner."

Peggy wanted to end the conversation quickly. She liked Jeff, but she wanted to wallow in self pity for a while. She missed Kent and wondered why he hadn't called her.

"Um, when?"

"Tomorrow night?"

"I don't know."

"We didn't get a chance to say goodbye at the hotel and it would be great to catch up. I enjoyed your company immensely, and we seemed to hit it off. I'd really like to see you again."

Peggy sighed. She didn't want to appear rude and brush him off. Jeff was a decent guy and she liked him, she just didn't feel like socializing right now. She remained silent, trying to decide how to let him down gently.

"Peggy?"

"Yes?" She grimaced, knowing he could tell she didn't want to have dinner with him.

"Is something wrong? Did I do something to change your mind about me?"

"No," Peggy blurted. "I'm going through something at the moment and don't feel like going out with anyone."

"You know, going out might be the best way to get over your blues."

Peggy thought about that for a moment. She realized she couldn't sit around moping over Kent indefinitely. For all she knew she may never see him again. "I suppose you're right."

"You know I am. Come on, love, what have you got to lose?"

She sighed. "All right. When and where? I'll meet you there."

"Would you mind if I picked you up? That would be the gentlemanly thing to do."

"You have my address?" Her mind was still on Kent.

"Well, yes, it's in the phone book along with your name and number."

Peggy felt stupid. Of course it was in the phone book.

"Maybe you'd like to talk about it over dinner. Get it off your mind."

"What time do you want to pick me up?" She didn't want to get into it right now.

"Say, round seven?"

"Okay, see you then."

"I'm looking forward to it." He rang off.

Peggy sat the phone on the coffee table, stared at it and sighed. *Why haven't you called, Kent?*

Eleven

Jeff arrived at Peggy's home just before seven. When she opened the door, he was standing on the porch with a bunch of apricot roses in his hand. He handed her the bouquet, leaned in and kissed her cheek. Peggy's body tensed and she knew he'd felt it. She had spent part of the day moping around and the rest trying on different outfits, wondering where they'd be going for dinner. She hoped she wasn't over-dressed.

"You look lovely. It's great to see you again," Jeff said.

"Thank you. You look very handsome. But you always dress well." She stepped aside to let him in, then closed the door and headed for the kitchen to put the beautiful roses in water. Jeff followed. Peggy pulled a crystal vase from a cupboard underneath the sink, filled it with water and arranged the flowers. "These are gorgeous," she said, glancing over her shoulder at him. "And my favorite color, too." He had actually listened.

"They're not as lovely as you, Peggy." Jeff moved up behind her and slid an arm around her waist. She jumped at his unexpected touch.

"I'm sorry," she said, breathless. "You startled me." She attempted to smile.

Jeff gazed into her eyes and frowned. "Are you all right? You seem … jittery."

"It's nothing. I'm fine." She continued setting the flowers in water. "Where are we going for dinner?" She tried to relieve the tension between them.

"I thought we might drive down the coast and have dinner at the hotel."

"The Versace?" She slid the vase further onto the sink and turned around. "Why?"

"Why not?" He stepped closer. "We had a great time there, and I'm still a guest. Although, not for long. I'm being housed out here for a while."

"Really?" Peggy was backed up against the sink and couldn't move away from him. "Are you going to be working here for long?"

"Yes. I think it'll be good for my career. I could be here for a couple of years, or more." He leaned in and kissed her gently on the lips. Peggy's emotions gave way and she kissed him back, missing Kent.

When she realized what she was doing, she pulled away. "I'm sorry, that shouldn't have happened."

"I'm glad it did. I like you. And I'd like to get to know you better." He slid his arms around her and pulled her closer.

The heady scent of his aftershave made her body shiver. "Please, Jeff, don't."

"What's wrong? I thought you liked me."

Peggy wouldn't look at him. "I do like you, but…"

"Not in that way. I understand."

She felt terrible for hurting his feelings. "I'm not ready for a serious relationship with anyone right now."

He lifted her face up to meet his gaze. "I'm not asking you to marry me, just to go out and see what happens." He smiled. It was a genuinely nice smile.

Peggy's tense feelings lightened. She smiled back. "I'm being too intense, aren't I?"

"You have a right to protect your feelings. No one likes to get hurt."

Why did he have to be so understanding? Peggy sensed his feelings were hurt, but he was being incredibly generous about the whole situation. She admired him for that.

"Thank you. I appreciate you understanding."

He stepped away from her. "Shall we get going?"

"Yes." She moved past him and picked up her evening bag and a light cardigan.

Jeff opened the front door and waited for her to step outside. He followed her out and walked ahead of her down the path. Peggy caught up to him and he opened the car door for her.

The drive to the coast was silent at first, and Peggy had the impression that Jeff was still hurt by her reaction to him. She felt guilty. If she'd met him at any other time, they may well have started a relationship. Jeff had most of the qualities she was looking for, and she knew he was a decent man. She realized he had feelings for her and that he was in the same position she was with Kent, and it made her feel even worse. She never meant to hurt him.

Jeff glanced at her, the shadows of the lighted highway playing across her face made her look sad. He could see her mind was elsewhere, and he wanted her attention on him. He wanted a relationship with her, but didn't want to pressure her. He knew Kent Reynolds had something to do with the way she was feeling, and if he wasn't careful he might lose the opportunity to have her in his life. He decided to play it safe.

"Nice evening, isn't it?"

Peggy turned to look at him. "Yes, yes it is."

"Not much further now."

"Mm." She nodded.

"Are you hungry?" He tried to keep the mood light.

"A little. Maybe I'll have more of an appetite once we're there."

"I hope so, the food's delicious."

"Yes, it is. And the restaurant is lovely."

"Well, then, we'll fit right in, won't we?" He smiled. He was an attractive man, and his eyes reflected genuine sincerity. Something she liked about him.

"Jeff?"

"Yes."

"I'm sorry I'm not myself at the moment."

"No need to apologize, love. You're allowed to feel the way you are. And I do understand."

Peggy glanced out of the passenger window and frowned at her reflection. He was being way too decent about the whole situation, and she was beginning to feel more than guilty.

Jeff reached across and patted her hand. "Don't be too hard on yourself. I'm fine. If I wasn't I wouldn't be here."

Peggy tried to lighten her mood. She wanted to enjoy the evening. "Thank you." She gave a half smile.

"Oh, come on, you can do better than that."

She felt the corners of her mouth turning up. It was

odd, but Jeff had a way of making her smile. He had successfully managed to do it the day they'd had lunch in the Hinterland, when she was feeling blue over Kent.

"Look at that, you can smile. And a beautiful smile it is too."

Jeff found a parking space on the street, and turned off the engine. This would have been the perfect time to lean in and kiss her, but he didn't. Instead, he got out of the car, opened her door and held out his hand.

Peggy placed her hand in his, and he helped her out of her seat. His hand felt warm and safe. She liked that. He closed the door, keeping her hand in his. "Shall we go in?"

As she perused the menu, Peggy realized her appetite had returned. She glanced up and noticed Jeff watching her from across the table with a smile on his face.

"Found something you like?"

Peggy shifted in her chair, feeling self-conscious. Why would she feel that way about Jeff watching her?

"I think I'll be daring and try the quail. I've never had it before." She smiled at him, then frowned. "I hope that's all right? It's quite expensive."

"It's fine, love. Have anything you like."

"Thank you. You're a true gentleman."

"Would you like something to drink?"

Peggy didn't want to drink alcohol. "Juice is fine for me, thanks."

Jeff had the distinct feeling she was trying to avoid drinking anything alcoholic. Was she concerned he would try to get her drunk and take advantage of her? That would never happen. He respected her too much to do anything that stupid. "I don't think one drink would hurt. What if I order champagne?"

"Don't waste your money. To be honest, I really don't like the taste of champagne."

"All right, juice it is."

They talked and laughed throughout dinner and Peggy's blues had all but disappeared. She enjoyed being with Jeff again, and no thoughts of Kent had disrupted their evening together. By the time they ordered coffee, it was quite late. Patrons were thinning, and fatigue washed over Peggy. Jeff noticed her sparkle dissipating and thought about asking her to stay. Not with him, of course, there were two bedrooms in his suite.

"Peggy?"

"Yes?"

"I was thinking."

"What about?"

"Well, now, before you jump to conclusions hear me out, okay?"

"All right." Peggy gave him a dubious frown. "What were you thinking?"

"That, perhaps, you might stay over…"

Peggy shook her head.

"Just wait a minute."

"No," she said firmly.

"I have two bedrooms in my suite. You're welcome to use the spare." He smiled. "I wasn't suggesting we sleep together."

Peggy blushed. "Oh?"

"I did say don't go jumping to conclusions, didn't I?" he said, amusement in his eyes.

"Yes, you did and I apologize." She felt her face grow warmer.

"Apology accepted." He stood up and held out his hand. "Shall we?"

Peggy took his hand and stood up. "All right," she said, a small tremor in her voice. Should she stay the night or go home? She was tired, and it was a reasonable drive back.

"You can lock your door, love, but there's really no need." He squeezed her hand.

Whenever Jeff took her hand, she felt safe and protected. She knew he wouldn't try anything. She knew she could trust him.

"It's almost midnight. We'd best be going."

"Which room are you in?"

"One of the poolside suites."

Jeff led her by the hand through the hotel lobby. They walked along the dimly lit hallway and stopped outside one of the rooms. "Here we are." He unlocked the door, pushed it open, and motioned for her to go in ahead of him.

Peggy's stomach tightened as she stepped through the doorway. She glanced around the suite with nervous eyes, pulling her cardigan around her shoulders.

Jeff stepped inside and closed the door. He moved up behind her and turned her around to face him. "Peggy, relax." He gave her a reassuring smile.

"I … I will." She gazed around the room. "Where's the spare room?"

He pointed across the living room. "Over there." He walked over, opened the door and flicked on the light. Peggy followed. "I hope you'll be comfortable."

The room was lovely. "I'm sure I will be."

Jeff wanted to kiss her, but didn't dare. He knew if he did, Peggy would get the wrong idea about him asking her to stay. He reached for her hand and kissed it instead. "Well, goodnight, love. Sleep well."

Peggy watched him walk to his room and open the door. "Jeff?"

He turned around. "Yes?"

"Thank you. It's been a lovely evening. Just what I needed."

Jeff smiled at her. "You're welcome." He stepped into his room and closed the door.

Peggy closed her door, but didn't lock it. She knew she had nothing to worry about.

Twelve

I t was 1.54 a.m. and Peggy lay staring at the bedside clock wondering why she couldn't sleep. She'd had a lovely evening with Jeff and realized she liked him very much. She also had to admit that while she'd been with him, all thoughts of Kent had completely vanished from her mind.

She turned over, plumped her pillows and tried to get comfortable. Staring at the closed bedroom door, she thought about her current circumstances. Should she forget about Kent and try to make something from the new relationship that was forming with Jeff? At least he was here, and planning to stay for a while. He was a genuine, kind-hearted man, and he cared for her. That's more than she could say for Kent Reynolds. He hadn't even bothered to contact her since his return to the States.

Peggy sighed, flopped onto her back and stared at the ceiling. She was vulnerable, she knew. She had been alone for so long she wanted a man in her life again. Not that she was desperate, she wasn't, but she missed the familiarity and intimacy that came with a good relationship. And she missed the sex.

At dinner one evening, some of her close friends had joked that, after such a long time without a man, she was a virgin again. They suggested she buy herself a vibrator, one friend offering to pay for it. Peggy told them she preferred a warm male body attached to that kind of appendage, and everyone laughed. To her it wasn't a joke. She did prefer a man to a battery operated device, and she knew there was a real flesh and blood male sleeping in the next room who wanted a relationship with her.

Peggy reached across and flicked on the lamp, then pushed back the sheet and got out of bed. She walked over to the window, folded her arms across her chest, and gazed outside—the night sky was sprinkled with a multitude of glittering stars.

What was she doing? Kent may never come back to Australia. He may latch on to some Hollywood bimbo and never give her a second thought. Jeff was here, and from what she could tell, was falling for her. She liked him, and knew it wouldn't be difficult to fall in love with him in time.

She padded across the room and opened the door. A solitary, cream-colored lamp on the sofa table shed a soft, warm glow across the, otherwise, dark room. Peggy walked into the living room and gazed across at Jeff's door. Should she knock? Should she tell him how she felt?

Just as Peggy contemplated what she should do, Jeff's door opened and he stepped into the room. He was wearing a hotel robe, and his hair was loose around his shoulders.

"Hey, love, can't sleep?" He closed the door, padded across the room to her and rubbed her arm. He hadn't been able to sleep either, and had been lying in bed thinking about her sleeping in the next room. He headed to the kitchen. "Want some warm milk?"

Peggy turned around and watched him in the kitchen. "Sure, I'm up for anything that will help me sleep, right about now." Realizing how that must have sounded, she bit her lip and looked at the floor. Was that a Freudian slip? Was she subconsciously thinking about sex with Jeff?

He looked across the room at her, an eyebrow raised and an amused smile on his face. "Be careful how you word things, love. You wouldn't want me to get the wrong idea, would you?" He opened the refrigerator.

Peggy gave him a furtive glance. "Maybe that's exactly what I mean."

Jeff closed the refrigerator and walked across the room. He rested a hand on her shoulder and stared into her eyes. "What are you saying?"

Peggy's gaze shifted to her bare feet, but Jeff pushed a finger under her chin and raised her face up to meet his questioning stare.

"I … think I'm saying I want to be with you."

"Don't rush into anything, love. You may wake up and regret it in the morning, and I don't want to be that regret." He pulled her into his arms and held her. "We have plenty of time." He wanted to kiss her, touch her, but he knew she was vulnerable and he didn't want to be that guy.

Peggy eased herself out of his arms and frowned at him. "I wouldn't regret it."

Jeff smiled and stroked her hair. "Yes, you would. You need time to get over what's going on with you right now, not jump into bed with me. That won't solve anything."

"Any other man would take advantage of the situation."

"I'm not any other man." He leaned in to her. "I really like you, and I don't want to ruin what *could be* by doing something rash." He took her by the hand and led her to the sofa. Peggy sat down. "Kent Reynolds is behind these feelings of yours, isn't he?"

"How did you know?"

"He hurt you in some way?"

"Yes." She didn't want to make Jeff feel bad by telling him how she felt about Kent, but she had no choice. "I thought I was in love with him, but now I'm not sure."

"Why?" Jeff sat beside her.

Peggy glanced at him sideways. "Because of you."

Jeff's heart soared. She did have feelings for him. "What do you mean?"

She sighed. "You are a really nice man. Every time we've been out together you've treated me like a lady."

"As you should be treated." He smiled and took her hand in his.

Peggy gave a thin smile. "That's just it."

"What?"

"Kent treated me badly. He slept with other women, and acted like I was hired help." She frowned. "Okay … I was hired help, but he knew how I felt and he still did those things."

"Maybe he didn't know how to deal with it."

Peggy glowered at him. "Are you defending him?"

Jeff rubbed her hand. "No, love, not at all. But he is a celebrity, and they live very different lives to the rest of us ordinary folk. He may not know how to love someone honestly."

She thought about that. It made sense. But it still didn't change the fact that she deserved to be treated better. Jeff treated her with caring and respect and she appreciated that about him. She rested her hand on top of his. "I meant what I said. I need to be with you. I'm not doing this on the rebound."

Jeff shook his head. "I know you think it's what you want, but it's not. Not now, anyway. Not until you're sure of how you feel."

Peggy was offended. He'd wanted to start something in her kitchen the previous evening, and she wondered why he didn't now. "You wanted me last night, why not now?"

He sighed and gave her a serious frown. "Yes, I did. But that was before I realized you had feelings for Kent."

"But I don't think I do."

"Yes, you do."

"I think what I felt for him might have been infatuation. We were living in close quarters, and he was parading around in his underwear most of the time." The image of Kent in those body-hugging black boxers popped into her head, and she shivered.

"Don't minimize your feelings. You need to deal with them." He leaned in, kissed her on the forehead and stood up. "I'm going to bed. You should do the same."

Peggy gazed up at him. "Mm. See you in the morning."

She did understand why Jeff had said no. He was a good man and he wasn't about to take advantage of her vulnerability. That made her even more confused about her feelings for him.

Next morning, Peggy was awakened by a knock on the door. She sprang up in bed, taking a moment to gather her sleepy thoughts and remember where she was.

"Are you awake, love?" Jeff's asked through the closed door.

Peggy blinked back the haze of sleep and ran her fingers through her hair. "Yes, I am. Come in."

The door swung open and Jeff entered the room, carrying a tray. "Morning, love." He set it down on her lap. "I thought you could do with a bit of pampering."

Peggy perused the tray, then looked up at him. "Thank you. This is lovely." He had ordered scrambled eggs, bacon, and cooked tomatoes, with a side of lightly buttered toast, a glass of freshly squeezed orange juice and a cup of black coffee. He had also managed to acquire a dusty pink Gerbera, another of her favorite flowers.

Jeff walked to the open doorway. "Enjoy."

Peggy frowned. "What about you?"

"I've already eaten. I let you sleep in for a bit before bringing in your brekkie."

She glanced at the clock. "It's nine o'clock?"

He smiled. "Yes. Do you have to be somewhere?"

"Well, no, but..."

"Then, enjoy." Jeff walked out of the room, leaving the door open.

Peggy rushed her breakfast. She knew she should spend more time appreciating his efforts, but she wanted to talk to him. She finished the last mouthful of coffee, pushed back the covers and got out of bed. She snatched her robe from the foot of the chair, slipped into it and walked out to the living room.

Jeff was sitting at the table reading the morning paper and drinking a mug of tea. He glanced up as she came toward him. "That was quick," he said.

"Sorry, I know I should have enjoyed it more, but I really need to talk to you."

Jeff stood up as Peggy reached the table and waited for her to sit down.

"Talk to me about what?"

Peggy sighed. She wasn't sure where to begin. She wanted to tell Jeff that she had come to the conclusion she wanted a relationship with him. There was no point in waiting for Kent. It seemed he'd gone back to the States and forgotten about her. She wasn't getting any younger, and she wanted a man in her life. One that would care for her, and he was that man. "Jeff, I want to be with you."

"You're not ready to commit to a relationship with me. We both know that."

"But I am." She reached across the table and rested her hand on his. "You're the kind of man I want to share my life with. You're kind, gentle, considerate, and you're a good man. You're everything I'm looking for."

Right at that moment, Jeff knew he was in love with her and wanted her to be in love with him. Problem was, Kent Reynolds wasn't out of her system, and Jeff wasn't sure that he ever would be. Could he play second fiddle to the actor? It wasn't a position he wanted to be in, but because of his feelings for her he might not have a choice. He could bear it if there was a glimmer of hope that one day she may truly come to love him.

"Are you sure, love?" Jeff stood up.

Peggy stood up and walked over to him. "Yes, I'm sure," she said, reaching up and pushing stray strands of his dark blond hair from his face.

Jeff couldn't resist any longer, he pulled her to him and kissed her. Peggy wrapped her arms around him and they kissed for a long time, the yearning inside each of them finally giving way.

When the kiss ended, Jeff eased Peggy away from him. He stared into her eyes, looking for any sign of love. There was definitely something, but he wasn't sure it was love. Lust more likely. "Peggy?"

"Yes?"

"What do you want to do about all this?" He stroked her hair and continued gazing into her eyes. His feelings were in turmoil. He wanted to remain the compassionate, understanding guy, but, right now, he also wanted to take her to bed and make love to her more than anything else he'd ever wanted before.

"What do you mean?" She frowned at him.

"Do you want to take it slow? Do you want to go to my room? What do *you* want?"

Peggy stepped backward. "I want…" She remembered that she'd tried to initiate them sleeping together in the early hours of the morning, and now Jeff wanted to know if she was going to act on it. "I want to make love with you." She pressed her body against his and he wrapped his arms around her, breathing in the sweet scent of her hair.

He could feel her hesitation, even though he didn't want to admit it, and wondered what he should do to alleviate her doubt. He held her for some time before speaking. Finally, he raised her face up to meet his gaze and asked, "Are you absolutely sure this is what you want? There's no going back once it's done, you know?"

"I know. I'm sure," she said, leaning in to him and trailing kisses up the side of his neck.

Jeff closed his eyes and drifted into the moment. Peggy's mouth on his skin felt incredible. She was tantalizing his senses and he could feel his attraction for her growing. He sighed, and moved her away from him. "Peggy, please. Stop."

She frowned. "Am I doing something wrong?"

He smiled. "No. You're doing everything right. But I need to ask you again … are you sure about this?"

Peggy gave him a seductive smile and unbuttoned his shirt. "Very sure." She trailed slow kisses up his chest to his neck and nuzzled his ear.

Jeff could stand it no longer. He took her hand and led her to his room. This time, there was no hesitation in her.

Thirteen

K ent opened his eyes, blinking back the brightness,
and gazed at his unfamiliar surroundings, wondering
where he was. He was lying in bed and his head
pounded the way it did when he woke up with a massive
hangover. As his hazy thoughts became clearer, he
realized he was in a hospital room, filled with bunches of
flowers, brightly-colored balloons, stuffed toy animals and
get well cards. He frowned at them for a moment and then
attempted to sit up. The throbbing ache in his head
transformed into a shooting pain and he fell back against
the mound of pillows.

When he reached up to examine his aching, bandaged
head, he felt some resistance, something was attached to
his hand. A drip stand with two plastic bags of fluid
hanging from it stood on the left side of the bed. He
frowned at the stand, then at his hand. His left leg felt
constricted, and when he ran his gaze down the bed he
could see that his leg was in a plaster cast in traction. Why
was he here? What had happened?

Kent glanced over at the bedside table, the buzzer was
sitting on top. He reached across, picked it up and held his

finger on the button. He needed to know what was going on.

Within seconds, the door snapped open and a matronly, mature-aged nurse entered the room. She appeared to be in her late fifties, with severe features and her hair pulled back in a tight knot. "So, you're finally back in the land of the living, Mr. Reynolds." She closed the door and walked over to the bed. "What can I do for you?"

"How did I get here?" Kent thought for a moment. "How long have I been here?"

"You were involved in an accident on the way from the airport. You've been here for over a month."

Kent couldn't believe it. "Five weeks? Which hospital is this?"

"Cedars Sinai."

A sickening feeling washed over Kent as he realized Peggy would have been waiting for his call. She'd think he had returned to his old way of life and forgotten all about her. "I need a phone."

"Mr. Reynolds, you're recovering from some serious injuries. What you need to do right now is rest."

"Look, I need a phone. Have one brought to me now."

The nurse stood at the foot of Kent's bed, her stern gaze remaining on him. "Mr. Reynolds, you really must calm down."

"I don't want to calm down. I want a phone NOW!"

"I'll go get the doctor. We may need to sedate you." The nurse turned around and walked briskly to the door, opened it and disappeared into the corridor.

"Just get me a Goddamn phone!" Kent yelled.

After several minutes, the door opened and an African-American doctor entered the room.

"I don't know what that nurse told you, but all I want is a telephone. I need to call someone. It's important."

"Mr. Reynolds, I'm Dr. Washington. You've been unconscious for more than a few weeks and you have to understand…"

"No. You have to understand that I need to make an urgent phone call right now." Kent raised himself onto an elbow and glared at the heavy-set man.

The doctor sighed. "If I allow you to make the call will you promise to settle down?"

"Yes." Kent slumped back against the pillows as a pain shot through his ribcage.

"Very well. I'll have one of our service team connect a telephone for you. But I want you to stay calm, otherwise I *will* keep you sedated. Am I clear on that?"

Kent didn't want to be sedated. That was the last thing he needed. "Yes, very clear. I just need to make this call, it's extremely important."

The doctor eyed him with concern. "Someone will bring you a phone shortly. In the meantime, you lie there and take it easy. Understood?"

The actor sighed. "Fine. Thank you."

"After you've made your call, I'll be back to take a look at you." The doctor left the room.

Kent lay in bed staring at the ceiling. How could this have happened? He had promised Peggy he'd call her the minute he arrived back in the US. After this length of time, she'd think he hadn't cared about her at all and that he'd just been trying to do what he had a year ago … get her into his bed.

"God, how could everything get so screwed up?" He sighed.

The door opened and a guy in a maintenance uniform strutted across the room to the bedside table. He set a telephone on top. "Hello, Mr. Reynolds, here's your phone." He plugged it in and checked to make sure it was working. "All ready to go."

Kent wouldn't be able to reach the phone from where it was. "Would you mind passing it to me, please?"

"Sure, no problem." The guy picked up the telephone and sat it on the bed beside Kent. "Need anything else?"

"No. Thanks." Kent smiled.

"Ok then." The guy walked across to the door then turned around. "My daughter's a big fan. Could I get your autograph for her?"

Kent wanted to make the call to Peggy, but didn't want to seem pretentious and rude, bad for his already declining reputation. "Sure. Got a pen and some paper?"

The maintenance guy pulled a notebook out of his shirt pocket and unclipped his pen. "Gee, thanks Mr. Reynolds. I know she'll be thrilled." He passed the book and pen to the actor.

"Who do I make it out to?"

"Oh, yeah. Melissa. She's seen every movie you've ever been in."

Kent scribbled a salutation and signature onto a page in the notebook and passed it back. "Well thank her for me. I really appreciate it."

The guy's smile widened. "I'll do that." He walked across to the door and left.

Kent stared at the phone for some time. What was he going to say to her? Maybe the truth for starters.

He leaned across the bed and opened the top drawer of the bedside table, looking for his wallet. Kent picked it up and flipped it open, hoping the note paper was still inside. He found the piece of paper, unfolded it and ran his finger over the neat handwriting.

It was just after eleven o'clock in the morning in LA and he wondered what time it would be in Queensland? He thought about the time difference and calculated that it would be around six or seven in the morning the next day there.

He dialed Peggy's number.

The phone rang continuously and Kent thought she wasn't going to answer. He was about to hang up when he heard a click on the other end of the line.

"H … Hello?" Peggy said in a sleepy voice.

"Peggy, it's Kent."

"Kent!" She jolted awake and frowned at the blurred red numerals on the clock. She rubbed her eyes. 5.05 a.m.

"Before you berate me for not calling, there's something you should know."

"What?" she asked, her voice tight. She expected some lame excuse, and was hurt by his non-communication for the past few weeks.

"I'm in the hospital and…"

"Oh, my God! What happened? Are you all right?"

"I was involved in an accident coming back from LAX. I've been lying in the hospital unconscious. The minute I came to, I asked for a phone so I could call you."

Peggy flicked on the lamp and jumped out of bed. "Why didn't someone contact me? Is there anything I can do?"

The brightness in the room woke Jeff and he turned over, squinting back the glare. "What is it, love? Who's on the phone?"

"Just a minute." Peggy covered the mouth piece with her hand. "It's Kent. He's been in the hospital all this time. He was involved in a car accident."

Jeff sat up. "Ah, I see."

Peggy gave him a furtive glance. "Please don't look at me like that."

"How do you want me to look?" Jeff got out of bed, pulled on his boxers and walked to the door. "Finish your call. I'll be out in the living room."

Peggy felt her heart turn to lead. She was so confused. She didn't want to hurt Jeff, but now she knew Kent hadn't forgotten about her.

She removed her hand from the receiver and could hear Kent's voice. "Peggy, what's going on?"

"Nothing, I just needed a minute, that's all," she lied. "This is so much to take in … it's such a shock."

"I know. I'm sorry. It was a shock for me, too. I woke up and the first person I wanted to talk to was you. Have you missed me?"

"Of course I've missed you. I wondered why you never called, but now I know." Peggy paced. She gazed across the room at the open door and wondered what Jeff was thinking. He had been so good to her—understanding, loving, kind and never once pressured her into anything. In fact, he was her logic … her rock.

"Can you come to the States?"

Peggy stopped pacing. She hadn't expected Kent to ask her to travel to the States to be with him. "You want me to come over there?"

"Yes. I really need you right now. You'd be good for my recovery. And besides all that, I miss you."

Jeff appeared in the doorway. The expression on his

face said everything. He was hurt. "You should go, love. It's something you need to do."

"Just a minute, Kent." She put her hand over the mouth piece. "Jeff?"

"I'm serious. You should go."

"But…"

"You need to sort out your feelings." He gave her pained look. "And I need to go." He walked into the room, picked up his clothes off the chair and began dressing.

"Jeff, I don't want you to go. Please, will you at least wait until I'm off the phone?"

"Why, love? So you can talk yourself out of how you feel about Kent, or talk me into staying with someone who doesn't love me."

"I do love you."

Jeff tried to smile. "I thought you could, but it's obvious you still have strong feelings for Kent. You need to make a decision about who you want to be with." He wondered if it was Kent she thought about when they made love.

"Jeff."

He sighed. "I really should go." He walked over and kissed her forehead. "I'll see you when you get back." With that said, he walked out of the room.

Peggy rushed to the doorway and saw the front door closing. Tears welled in her eyes. She didn't want Jeff to go. She remembered Kent on the other end of the line. "Kent?"

"Why do you keep covering the phone?"

"I … I needed a minute to get my head around everything you've told me. It's so unbelievable."

"Will you come?" Kent wanted an answer.

"I don't know. I have to work and…"

"I'm sure you can be put work on hold for a while. The company does have other drivers."

"Well, yes, but…"

"I really need to see you. Please, will you come?"

Peggy was torn between her feelings for Jeff and her feelings for Kent. She wanted to see Jeff before she left. There was her answer. She'd unconsciously made the decision to go.

"When do you want me to come over?"

"As soon as you can. I'll get my assistant to organize the flight and the hotel and someone will call you back with the details."

"I have something I have to do first. Can it be in a couple of days?"

There was silence on the other end of the phone.

"All right. Do what you have to do first, and I'll tell my assistant to book for Friday. I can't wait to see you."

Peggy wasn't sure how to feel. She wanted to be happy that Kent wanted to see her again, but she knew it would be at the expense of Jeff's feelings. Maybe the Universe was trying to tell her Jeff was the man she should be with and that Kent would be no good for her. She had already been the recipient of his moodiness, and hurt by his over-inflated ego and sex drive. Jeff would never do anything like that to her.

"Peggy, are you there?"

"Yes, I'm here."

"I'd better get some rest. The doctor's coming back to check on me soon. I'll see you Friday."

"All right. See you then." Peggy pressed the button and dropped the phone onto the bed. She threw on a pair of jeans, a stretch top and her boots, then rushed out to the living room, grabbed her car keys and headed out the door. She had to see Jeff.

Fourteen

There were roadworks on the freeway, and it took over half an hour for the banked up traffic to filter through. Peggy sat in her car dialing Jeff's cell phone, but he wouldn't pick up. By the time she pulled up outside the hotel dawn was breaking.

Peggy rushed along the hallway, heading to Jeff's suite. When she arrived at his door she raised her hand to knock but pulled back, feeling her stomach tighten. What could she say? Jeff had heard the telephone conversation. He knew Kent had asked her to fly to the States. How could she convince him to wait for her? Why should he when he knew she was running off to be with another man? She had to talk to him. Had to explain. She raised her hand again.

Just as she was about to knock, the door swung open and Jeff was standing in the doorway with a suitcase in his hand. "Peggy? I didn't expect to see you here."

Peggy glanced at the suitcase and the other luggage sitting by the door. "Where are you going?" Her heart felt heavy in her chest.

"I've decided not to take the job here. I'm heading back home." He wouldn't look her in the face.

Peggy stepped closer and Jeff moved aside. She entered the suite and closed the door. "Why would you do this? I thought…"

"So did I, love. I didn't think you'd be hopping on a plane and heading to LA today."

"I'm not leaving until Friday." Peggy frowned at him.

"But you are leaving." Jeff set the case down, walked over to the sofa and sat down.

"Yes, you told me I should go."

"I know I did. But I thought you'd make the right decision." He folded his arms across his chest.

Peggy crossed the room. "If you don't want me to go, say so."

"If I asked you to stay, would you?"

"I…" She had no answer to give him.

"That's what I thought." He stood up, walked over to her, pulled her to him and held her. "I love you. I thought, perhaps, you could love me too. I hoped you would. But now it seems you still have strong feelings for Kent."

Peggy slid out of his arms. "He's injured. What do you want me to do?"

"I want you to do what's right for you, love." He rubbed her arm, a sad look of loss evident on his face.

Peggy's feelings were conflicted. Her heart ached. She wanted to be with Jeff, but she also wanted to see Kent. She looked away, tears welling in her eyes.

Jeff pulled her into his arms and stroked her hair. He loved the smell of her hair and realized he may never get the opportunity to hold her again. He kissed the top of her head.

"I don't want you to leave. I want you to be here when I get back."

"Why?"

Peggy glanced up at him, tears spilling down her face. "Because I care for you."

"I know you do, but it's not enough."

"Please, Jeff, please wait for me."

He gazed into her glistening eyes and felt sadness. What happened if she decided to come back, pack up and move to the States? He would have waited for nothing. "How do you know how you'll feel, once you see Kent? What if you decide to move over there?"

"I don't think I will."

Jeff moved her away from him. "You don't know what's going to happen, and I can't wait around until you figure it out." He wanted to, he did, but he had to do what was right for him. And right now that was to head home and try to get over her.

"Please wait for me." Peggy pushed herself into Jeff's arms and held him tight.

He could feel a thick lump forming in his throat. He sighed and whispered in her hair, "I can't, love." He wanted Peggy to make a choice, but he wouldn't ask. He couldn't put that kind of pressure on her. "You'd best go. I need to get organized." He raised her chin to him and kissed her gently on the lips.

She sighed and wrapped her arms around his neck, pulling him to her. "Please, don't go."

Jeff eased her away from him again and looked into her eyes. "You're still in love with Kent, what hope do I have?"

"I don't know how I feel right now. That's why I'm going over there, to find out. Won't you please wait? I really need you to do that for me. You've been amazing.

You've been my rock and I don't want to lose you. Please, Jeff."

"My old nana used to say, 'You can't have your cake and eat it too.'"

Tears slid down her face again. "Please."

Jeff brushed the tears from her cheeks with his thumbs and stared into her eyes. He wasn't sure if he could handle being hurt again. His wife had run off with his best friend, which had been almost impossible to deal with. His boys had been the only stabilizing factor in his life at the time; otherwise he might not be here now. He had become mister mom to his sons, working from home on articles for newspapers and magazines. It had been a long time since he'd allowed himself to feel again—to be in any kind of relationship, and he wasn't sure if he wanted to put himself through something like that again. But seeing the look of anguish in Peggy's eyes made him give in.

He sighed. "All right. I'll wait."

A slight smile crept across Peggy's face. She leaned up and kissed him.

Jeff didn't try to pull away. It could be the last chance he'd have to kiss her. When the kiss ended, he held her at arm's length and stared into her eyes. Would he ever see the look of love there? He hoped so.

As Peggy drove back toward home, she couldn't help feeling excited about seeing Kent again. The feelings she'd felt when she was with him came flooding back. What if Jeff was right? What if Kent asked her to move to the States? Would she go? She had no idea what she was doing. She had a good man in her life now, why would she jeopardize that by flying to LA? Because she still had feelings for Kent, and because he was lying in hospital injured, she told herself.

When Peggy pulled up in her driveway a young man from a courier service was standing at her front door. She got out of her car, and walked over to him.

"Are you Peggy Anton?" he asked.

"Yes."

He pushed an envelope and an electronic signature pad into her hand. "Sign here, please."

Peggy signed, handed the device back and examined the envelope in her hand. When she looked up, the young man was almost at her front gate. "Thanks," she called. He continued out the gate, without looking back, and rode off on his bike. Peggy tore open the envelope, inside was flight confirmation and hotel reservation details. She was to leave at 3.30 p.m. Friday afternoon.

She opened her front door and stepped inside. There was so much to do before she left. Gary would have to be notified that she wouldn't be available to work. She had to organize for someone to pay her bills and collect the mail while she was away. She had to pack. How would she ever be ready in time?

Fifteen

LAX was chaotic. Peggy had never been inside such an enormous airport before; it was like a city all on its own. So overwhelming. After clearing border security, she was directed to the baggage claim area to pick up her luggage. That had been a drama in itself, when her bags were nowhere to be found for the first half hour. Now, she was waiting for someone to collect her from the pickup point. The note in the envelope said that Kent's PA would be here by the time Peggy arrived, but from where she was standing no one had come for her.

Peggy waited for over half an hour before calling Kent at the hospital.

"Kent Reynolds speaking."

"Kent, it's me."

"Peggy? Are you here?"

"Yes, I'm at the airport. No one's come to pick me up. I've been standing here for almost an hour now."

"Chelsea is there somewhere. She called before she left to let me know she was on her way to get you."

"Well, she's not here. I'm at the pick up point and…"

"I'll give her a call and call you right back. Don't go anywhere."

"I won't. I have no idea how to get to you, anyhow."

"I'll call you back." He rang off.

Peggy dropped her phone into her bag, folded her arms across her chest and sighed. She was tired, hungry, and in need of a shower and change of clothes. She'd been looking forward to her time in LA, but it wasn't starting out as she had hoped. There was a sudden tap on her shoulder, and she swung around. A young woman with long brown hair and a pleasant face was standing there.

"Hi, I'm Chelsea, Kent's personal assistant. Sorry about the mix up. I was waiting upstairs and we must have missed each other."

"Oh?" Peggy reached out to shake her hand. "I'm Peggy. It's nice to meet you."

"Can I give you a hand with those?" She looked at the luggage sitting at Peggy's feet. "The car is just along here." She pointed along the path. The third car in the line was a black JEEP Cherokee.

"Thanks, I'd appreciate it." Peggy grabbed the handle of the heaviest case and pulled it along behind her. Chelsea picked up the onboard bag and the duffel bag. They walked to the car and loaded the luggage into the back, then Chelsea opened the passenger door for Peggy and motioned for her to get in. Her phone rang and she pulled it from her bag. It was Kent.

"Hi, did Chelsea find you?"

"Yes, I'm just getting into the car now."

"Great. I'll see you soon."

"I'm looking forward to it."

Kent rang off.

Before long, they were leaving the airport and on their way to the hotel.

Chelsea seemed like a nice young woman, and Peggy wondered how she had come to work for Kent. She wanted to ask her, but didn't want to seem jealous or overly curious. It was Chelsea who started the conversation.

"Your first time in LA?"

"Yes, it is. It's been quite an experience so far." Peggy looked across at Chelsea and smiled.

"LAX can be like that, especially if you don't know your way around the airport."

"Mm, I can see that. It's huge."

"Are you planning on staying long?"

Peggy wondered why she would ask a question like that. Kent was in the hospital and no one knew exactly when he'd be released, and she had flown all this way to be with him while he recovered. "I don't know. Kent asked me to be with him while he recuperates, and who knows how long that could take."

"Oh, I didn't mean anything by the question, just making conversation." Chelsea glanced at Peggy sideways, then focused her gaze on the road again.

"I didn't think you did," Peggy lied. That's exactly what she'd thought.

"The hotel you'll be staying at is very nice. Everything right at your fingertips. It's not big and flashy, but I didn't think you'd want that from what Kent told me."

What had Kent said about her?

"Is it close to the hospital? As I don't have a car, I'd like to be able to walk there."

"It's a few blocks from Cedars Sinai."

"Oh, good. Thank you."

"My pleasure."

Peggy had the distinct feeling that Chelsea didn't like her. She wondered if, perhaps, Kent had had a thing with her at some time. It was more than likely, given his reputation. Peggy wished she had the courage to ask her straight out, but knew she didn't. She just had an unsettling feeling in the pit of her stomach about the young woman. Maybe when Kent was well enough she'd ask him.

The hotel was quaint and rather quirky. It wasn't big or flash, as Chelsea had said, but it had a certain bygone era charm. Once Peggy checked in and was in her room, she unpacked, got settled in, then went to take a much-needed shower. Afterward, she would get directions to the hospital and make her way there to visit Kent. She hadn't wanted to go there straight from the airport, she wanted to freshen up first, have a bite to eat and feel a little more energized before facing Kent lying in a hospital bed.

As Peggy strolled along the street, heading toward the hospital, she suddenly felt very alone. She was in a strange city, half way around the world, and knew no one other than Kent. She started thinking about her situation as she continued along the street.

What if Kent hadn't been involved in an accident? Would he have bothered to contact her, or would he have come back and got on with his life? And what about Chelsea, was she a spurned ex-lover? Was she angry that Peggy was in LA at Kent's request? To Peggy's mind it seemed that way.

Cedars-Sinai Medical Center was hard to miss. Peggy

stopped and gazed up at the expansive glass and concrete structure that appeared to overshadow the busy intersection. It seemed to her that Americans did everything big. She wandered across the hospital courtyard and into the building.

Peggy's stomach squirmed as she travelled up in the elevator. Was she doing the right thing by being here? The elevator stopped and the doors slid open. Peggy stepped out into the corridor and approached the nurses' station.

A nurse sitting behind the counter looked up at her. "Can I help you?"

"Yes. I'm looking for Kent Reynolds's room. He's expecting me." Peggy smiled at the woman.

"Peggy? Yes, he's been waiting for you. Anxiously, I might add." She smiled, stood up and moved around the counter. "If you'll follow me, I'll take you to his room."

Peggy followed her along the corridor and they stopped at the last door on the right. "You can go on in." She opened the door.

"Thank you." Peggy stepped through the doorway. The room resembled a five star hotel suite.

Kent heard her footsteps. "Peggy, is that you?" He held out his hand.

"Yes." She rushed across the room and almost fell into his arms. "How are you?" She pulled herself free and studied him for a moment.

"I'm hoping to get paroled any day now." He smiled.

"Are you sure that's wise? I mean, you were involved in a car accident and were unconscious for a few weeks."

"Hey, I'm not going to let a little thing like that keep me down for long."

Kent's head was bandaged and his handsome face

covered in fading yellow bruises and fine scratches. His left arm was also bandaged and his right leg was in a plaster cast with hospital staff signatures and drawings all over it.

"By the look of you, it would be better to stay here for a bit longer." Peggy frowned. "You don't want to risk complications."

"No way. I want to go home so that we can spend some time together. *Alone*." He reached for her hand.

"Kent."

"There's no point in trying to talk me into staying any longer than I have to, so don't try."

"All right." She sighed and smiled at him, her hand still in his. "It's really good to see you."

"It's great to see you. I've missed you."

"You have?"

"Of course I have. What did you expect? That I came back to LA and forgot about you?"

Peggy gave him a guilty look. She could feel her cheeks growing warm and knew she was blushing.

"You did, didn't you?" He let go of her hand, reached up and turned her face toward him. "Why, Peg? I said I'd call, and I would have, except I ended up here."

"I just got to thinking that you're a celebrity; wealthy, good-looking. You could have anyone you want, why would you even begin to bother with someone who lives so far away?"

"Because I care about you." He rubbed her cheek. "Don't you know that by now?" Peggy didn't answer. "I'm asking the doctor to let me out of here. The sooner we can spend some time together talking, the better."

"Please don't do anything that could jeopardize your recovery just because I'm insecure."

"Is that all it is, insecurity?" He cupped her cheek with his hand.

"I think so. You were gone and I was alone." Peggy suddenly felt a pang of guilt. How could she tell Kent that she'd started a new relationship, thinking he was never going to get in touch with her again? She decided not to think about it now. His recovery was all that mattered.

Two days later, Kent was released from the hospital. Chelsea arrived early to pick them up. She didn't seem at all pleased when he told her Peggy would be staying at his house. The drive to the Hollywood Hills was tense. Chelsea drove the Cherokee without entering into the conversation. Women only did that when they were angry about something. And Peggy knew what that something was—her.

The hospital had arranged for a private nurse to be with Kent for the next 48 hours, 'just to be on the safe side', Doctor Washington had said. Kent was not at all happy about it, but resigned himself to the fact that it was either that or another week in the hospital.

When they arrived home, he was taken to his room and put straight to bed. The nurse settled him in, checked his vitals and plumped his pillows. Then she asked to be shown to her room. Chelsea escorted her to one of the guest bedrooms, then came back to Peggy and showed her to her room, which was at the other end of the house.

After unpacking and changing into something comfortable, Peggy wandered through the house to Kent's room. She knocked before entering, in case the nurse was with him. She wasn't.

"Yes?" Kent's voice echoed through the door.

Peggy opened it and peered inside.

"Come in, honey. You don't have to knock." Kent sat the book he was reading on the bedside table and patted the bed beside him.

Peggy crossed the expansive room and sat down. "I wasn't sure if the nurse was here."

"No. I asked her for some time out. I'm sick of being prodded and poked."

"I can understand that. At least you don't have the drip in anymore." She glanced at his hand.

"Yes, that's something. That thing was uncomfortable." He frowned at the bandage on his hand, then looked at her. "You look very nice. How are you feeling? Has jet lag settled in yet?"

"Thank you. I'm tired, but no jet lag yet. I'm expecting it to catch up with me pretty soon though."

"Well, then, maybe you should lie down for a while." He gave her a cheeky smile and patted the empty side of his massive, king-sized bed.

Peggy smiled back. "I think you need to rest. I'd just be a distraction."

"And a very lovely distraction, too." He reached out and pulled her to him.

"Kent, don't. You might hurt yourself." She pulled away from him.

"What is it?" He studied her for a moment. "You seem different. What's wrong?"

"Nothing." She wouldn't look at him.

"Peggy, look at me."

"Why?"

"Because I asked you to." He reached out and turned her face to meet his gaze. "Tell me what's wrong."

"I told you, nothing's wrong."

"I thought you'd be all over me. I hoped you'd be all over me. I would certainly like to be all over you right now." He smirked.

"Kent!"

"It's the truth. Why would you be surprised by that? You know I want to be with you."

"I'm … I'm not surprised, but you're injured. You have to be careful until you've recovered." Jeff popped into her head. Could she betray him by sleeping with Kent? More than likely, if she didn't stop herself.

"Peggy?"

"Yes."

"I just want to hold you, touch you, kiss you, that isn't going to kill me."

"I know. It's just I…"

"You what?" Kent kept his hand on her chin so she couldn't turn away.

"I don't want you to hurt yourself." She pointed at his plaster cast. "Look at you, you're bruised and plastered. If we started fooling around you could do something to yourself."

"Well, I'll take full responsibility for any injury I cause myself. How's that?"

"Kent, don't joke. This is serious."

All of a sudden he pulled her into his arms and kissed her. Peggy's head swam. She'd once dreamed of the time when he would kiss her like this, but now it felt wrong. She tugged herself free.

Kent frowned at her in frustration. "What is it?"

"I can't do this right now. I'm sorry." She stood up and headed for the door.

"Where are you going?"

"I think I need some sleep, my nerves are frayed. I'll see you in the morning." She opened the door and rushed out of the room, feeling guiltier than ever.

Sixteen

J eff was working on an article on his laptop when the phone rang. He turned around and glanced across the room. What time was it? He gazed at the computer's clock. 12.01 a.m. Who would be calling him at this hour? He pushed back his chair, picked up the phone and pressed the button. "Hello?"

"Hi, it's me."

"Peggy! I didn't expect to hear from you so soon. How are you, love? Is everything all right? How's Kent? God, it's good to hear your voice." He walked back to his desk and sat down.

"I'm fine. I got here three days ago. It's a huge city. I'm not used to it. Kent's at home now. He's laid up with a broken leg and some scrapes and bruises, but apart from that, he's doing fine. How are you? What have you been doing? It's good to hear your voice too."

"I'm okay. I'm working on an article for the Courier Mail at the moment and that's why I'm still awake. My deadline's tomorrow morning. It's just after midnight here. What time is it there?"

"Um." Peggy turned to look at her bedside clock. "It's a little after seven in the morning, yesterday for you." She hesitated and bit her lip. "Jeff?"

The tone in her voice alerted him to what was coming. His stomach shrank into a tight knot. "Yes, love?"

"I think I'm going to be staying for a while."

"How long's a while?" He rested his head in his hand.

"I don't know could be a month or so. Kent needs my help at the moment. I'm really sorry. I don't know what else to do." Tears welled in her eyes and slid down her cheeks. She brushed at them with her free hand and tried not to sniffle.

"I see. So, are you saying it's over between us?"

"I'm … not sure." She pushed her hand over her mouth to stifle the sob stuck in her throat, threatening to escape. Telling Jeff that she had chosen Kent hurt like hell. Her heart ached. Was she making the right decision?

"I love you, Peggy, but I don't want to be hurt again."

"And I don't want to hurt you. I care about you so much."

"But you're staying in the States with him?"

"If you were injured, I'd be with you. It's not as though I'll be here permanently. I will be back, I'm just not sure when."

"What are you telling me? That you want me to wait around until you decide who you want to be with? If you ever decide." He could hear the sting in his voice and felt a pang of guilt. "I'm sorry, but I can't do that."

"All right," she said, her voice quiet. "If you don't want to wait until I get back, I'll have to accept that." The tears tumbled down her face and she couldn't speak.

There was silence between them for some time.

"Are you in love with him?" Jeff wanted to know, finally.

More silence. Peggy couldn't answer. Her throat ached as the tears continued to spill.

"Peggy?"

She covered the receiver for a moment and sniffed back the tears and the pain before answering. "Yes?" she whispered.

"Will you answer my question?"

"I don't know. I haven't been here long enough to find out how I feel. Everything's been such a rush, and with Kent injured…"

"You said you care for me, what does that mean?"

"It means exactly what I said." A knock on her bedroom door startled her. She glanced across the room. Who could it be? It couldn't be Kent, he was confined to bed. It must be Chelsea. "Jeff, I have to go. I'll call you again soon. Please be patient."

"I will for now, but I can't wait forever, love." He hated saying it. He wanted to wait, but not long enough to have his heart broken again.

"Thank you. I'll call you next week. All right?" She wanted to be sure he would still be there.

"All right. I'll wait for your call. Take care. Bye."

"You too. Bye."

Peggy pushed the button on the phone and slid it onto the bedside table. The knock came again. "Just a minute." She wiped her eyes, sniffed back the tears, got out of bed and opened the door.

Kent was in a wheelchair.

"Morning, Peg. Surprised?" He smiled up at her.

"Yes, I am. How…?"

"I arranged it with nurse misery. She's leaving, and I wanted a way of getting around the house without having to ask you to do everything for me." He pushed a button on the armrest and backed up.

"But I thought she had to be here until tomorrow afternoon."

"I wanted us to have some alone time. That's all right with you, isn't it?"

"Of course it is. I just want to be sure you'll be okay without medical assistance."

"I'll be fine. The cast will be coming off in a couple of weeks and I'll be a free man, then you'd better watch out." He gave her a cheeky smile and a wink.

"Let's take things slowly, all right? You're not out of the woods just yet. And I'm not about to do anything to jeopardize your recovery."

"Why don't you let me worry about my health, okay?" He reached out, grabbed her and pulled her onto his lap.

Peggy floundered, trying to keep her weight off his broken leg, but Kent wouldn't let her go. "Peg, it's all right. You won't hurt me." He held her in place.

"Kent, let me up … let me up now!"

"No." He struggled with her. "Will you relax? I just want to kiss you."

Peggy wasn't only concerned about hurting Kent physically; she was also concerned about hurting Jeff emotionally. She wasn't sure what to do about her confused feelings, and wasn't even sure what her feelings were. Kent wasn't about to back down. He wanted to take the relationship further, and he usually got what he wanted. Peggy knew she wouldn't be able to put him off for long. They really couldn't do anything with Kent's leg in a cast. At least that would give her more time to sort out her emotions.

Kent leaned in and kissed her. Peggy stopped squirming and drifted into the moment. He was an incredible kisser. He kissed like he was making love with his mouth: warm, sensual, and when he slipped his tongue in and gently massaged her tongue it sent a quiver through her abdomen all the way to her womanhood. Peggy wrapped her arms around his neck and the heated kiss continued.

Their passionate encounter was interrupted by the sound of someone clearing their throat behind them. Their lips parted.

"Well, this looks cozy," Chelsea said, her arms folded across her chest. "Aren't you meant to be getting some bed rest, Kent?"

"I've been paroled. The nurse organized this chair for me, and she's gone. I'm up and rearing to go." He gave her a sideward glance and a thin smile.

Chelsea wasn't amused. "You really should take things easy for a while. You wouldn't want to relapse and end up back in the hospital, would you?"

Peggy climbed off Kent's lap and straightened her hair and clothes.

"No chance of that. I'm feeling great … better than great, apart from this cast." He slapped the plaster. "Once this thing comes off I'll be good as new." He winked at Peggy.

"Well, don't blame me if you hurt yourself." Chelsea turned on her heel and headed to the kitchen.

Kent glanced at Peggy; her face was flushed. "Don't worry about it, Peg, I can handle her."

"Why is she like that? It's me isn't it?"

"No. I'll tell you about it some time. In the meantime, why don't we have breakfast by the pool?" He reached for her hand.

"Kent?"

He lowered his hand and sighed. "What?"

"Did you and Chelsea have … a thing?"

He didn't answer.

"Kent?" Peggy walked over to him.

"It was a long time ago. A lifetime, in fact."

She crouched in front of him. "Then why is she here?"

"Just because we're not a couple anymore doesn't mean I should fire her, does it? She's very good at her job, and I appreciate her staying on as my assistant."

"I think she still has feelings for you." Peggy stood up.

"Our relationship ended three years ago. She has another man in her life now. Why would she still have feelings for me?"

"Trust me, Kent, she does. Maybe that's why she stayed on."

Kent scoffed at the idea. "That's ridiculous. You're reading way too much into it."

"Women can sense these things, and I'm telling you she does. Who ended the relationship?"

Kent glanced at her sideways. "Me. She wanted more than I was prepared to offer."

"Well, there you are." Peggy gazed along the hallway.

"You really think so?" He frowned.

"I know so."

Kent followed her gaze. "Then, perhaps it's time she got a better offer."

"What do you mean?"

129

"I know someone who's looking for an experienced personal assistant. I'll get in touch and suggest he give her a call."

Peggy was surprised. "You'd do that?"

"Of course I would. I don't want anyone coming between us, especially an ex-lover." He smiled and took her hand. "I'll make the call after breakfast."

The offer must have been too good to refuse. Chelsea was apologizing to Kent as she headed out the front door. She told him she needed to move on, her career had become stale and this was a great opportunity. She offered to moonlight, if Kent wanted her to, but he declined and wished her well.

Once she was gone, Kent headed back out to the pool. Peggy was taking a swim. He liked watching her. She swam the length of the pool and back, then climbed out. She was wearing a peach colored bikini, the kind that accentuated her assets. She wanted Kent to see how well she looked after her body. And he noticed.

"You look great in that," he told her, roaming her body with an eye of appreciation.

"Thank you. I try to take care of myself," she said, grabbing the towel off the back of a deck chair and drying herself.

"I can see that," Kent replied. He couldn't take his eyes off her. She had great curves and long legs. Something stirred in his groin and he moved the wheelchair up to the table to hide his reaction. He wished he could take her to bed right now, but that was something to look forward to when the cast came off.

"Want some juice?" Peggy picked up the jug and poured juice for herself.

"No, thanks, I'm good." He watched her move around the table and sit down. "Well, we have the house to ourselves now."

"Yes," she said, taking a sip of juice.

"What would you like to do?"

"Do you think we could go out?" She gazed across the valley. What an amazing view.

"Of course we can. I don't plan to sit around here for too long. I want to show you around LA."

"What about your leg?"

"It's fine. Stop worrying. I'll organize a car for us. We can go wherever you like."

"Could I drive?" Peggy asked. "I'd really like it to be just you and me."

"Do you think you can handle a left-hand drive?"

"Sure. It can't be that different, can it?"

"All right. We'll take the Porsche."

Peggy's mouth gaped in surprise. "You're letting me drive your Porsche?"

"Why not? You're a safe driver. I should know." He smiled.

Peggy jumped up, rushed around the table and eased herself onto Kent's lap. She kissed him hard on the mouth and said, "Thank you."

"No problem. If this is the kind of reaction I'm going to get, I'll have to do it more often." Kent's senses went into overdrive. He wanted to get up out of the chair, lift her into his arms and carry her to his bed. It frustrated the hell out of him that he couldn't, and it showed on his face.

"Is something wrong?" Peggy noticed his scowl.

He sighed. "It's not you, it's this whole *stupid* situation."

"What do you mean?"

"Look at you." He gestured at her swimsuit. "You're arousing the hell out of me and there's nothing I can do about it."

"There'll be plenty of time for all that once the cast comes off." She could feel his arousal beneath her, but didn't acknowledge it.

"I'm incapacitated. That doesn't stop me from feeling." He pulled her to him and kissed her.

Peggy melted into him, sliding one arm around his body and the other around his neck. Kent snuck a hand under her top and massaged her breast. Peggy moaned. Having Kent touch her that way made her realize she wanted more. She pulled her mouth from his. "Kent, stop. We can't."

"Why not? I think we could, if we're careful. You could be on top." His eyebrows rose and he gave her a cheeky grin.

Peggy thought about it for a moment. That could work. No! What was she thinking? Kent was recovering, and she needed to sort out her feelings before things got more complicated. But, she really wanted to be with him. See him naked. Touch him, kiss him, taste him, and feel him inside her. He would finally be hers. Peggy's stomach tightened with anticipation. He had almost made love to her in her dream, now he could in real life.

"Do you really think it could work? Me on top, I mean. I don't want to hurt you."

Kent frowned at her, surprised. "You wouldn't hurt me. Trust me. Are you saying what I think you're saying?"

She smiled and touched his face. "Yes. I think I am."

Peggy attempted to climb off Kent's lap, but he pulled her to him.

"No. Stay there." Kent turned the wheelchair around, maneuvered it through the doorway and headed toward his bedroom. He wanted to carry her, but as he couldn't this was the next best thing.

Seventeen

Felicity had been right about Kent. He really was an amazing lover. Even though his movements were restricted by the cast, he knew exactly how to please Peggy. He had been attentive and gentle, considering her every need. His mouth and hands had caressed, teased and explored every inch of her, setting her body on fire and her mind in a sensual daze. Their lovemaking had lasted long into the afternoon.

Peggy gave a contented sigh as she lay wrapped in Kent's arms. Her dream had come true. They had finally made love, and she was deliriously happy. No feelings of guilt. She was with the man she was meant to be with. She had finally admitted to herself that she was in love with him.

Kent stirred and woke up. "Hey, lovely lady, what time is it?"

She gazed into his sleepy, chocolate brown eyes and smiled. "It's a little after six."

Kent glanced over her shoulder at the bedside clock. "Man, I didn't expect to sleep this long."

Peggy touched his face and smiled. "That's ok. You're still recuperating, and you did expend a lot of energy today."

"You're right, I sure did." He leaned across, kissed her forehead and smiled. "And it was worth every ounce." He fell back onto his pillows. "Can I take you out for dinner?"

She sighed. "Could we order in? I'd like to stay here tonight, if that's ok?"

Kent smiled. "Of course it's ok. We have a lot of catching up to do." He gave her a cheeky wink.

Peggy gave him a playful slap. "Stop that. Haven't you had enough? We were at it all day." She smiled and blushed.

"I could never have too much of you." He pulled her to him and kissed her. His stomach growled loudly and broke the mood. They both looked at each other and burst into laugher.

"Sorry about that. I guess my stomach's trying to tell me we skipped lunch. So, what would you like to order for dinner? You can have anything your heart desires."

Peggy glanced at him sideways, a mischievous smile spreading across her face.

Kent got her meaning. "You can have that later, for dessert."

"You pick. I'm sure you know what's good in LA."

"Indeed, I do. Give me the phone."

The Chinese takeout Kent had ordered was delicious. Peggy had had Chinese food before, but nothing like the dishes that had been delivered. It seemed that everything in LA was done on a grand scale. She sighed.

Kent dropped his chopsticks into the empty container and looked at her. "Something on your mind?"

Peggy jabbed her chopsticks into her food and slid the container onto the table. "I was just thinking how wonderful it is being here with you." She gazed at her surroundings. "This house. The amazing view. The wonderful food. And most importantly, you. What more could a woman ask for?" She gave him a half smile.

"But?" He looked at her, his eyebrows knitting into a frown.

"I guess I've just realized that I can't stay here forever. I'll have to go back home some time. What then?"

Kent gave a heavy sigh. He didn't want to think about it or discuss it right now. They'd been having a great time, why spoil it? "Don't think about that tonight. Let's just enjoy the fact that we're here … together … now."

Peggy had also realized something else. Although Kent had made love to her, like he was in love with her, he hadn't actually said those three little words—those three very important words. She hadn't said 'I love you' either. She wanted to hear him say it first. She needed to hear him say those words.

She sighed and glanced out of the panoramic window at the distant city lights.

Kent leaned across and turned her face toward him. "What's really on your mind?"

"Nothing." Peggy moved his hand from her chin but didn't let it go.

"Come on, Peg, I think I know you well enough by now to know something's bothering you. What is it?"

"I don't want to spoil our time together. Just forget about it."

Kent rested his other hand on hers. "How can I, now that I know something's wrong? Talk to me."

"You really want to know?" She stared into those beautiful eyes. "Wouldn't you prefer to just have a good time and not make any rash promises or say…"

"Ah." It finally occurred to him. His expression turned somber.

Peggy frowned. "Ah, what?"

"I think I know what's on your mind." He tugged her hand. "Come here."

She stood up and moved around the table.

He pulled her onto his lap. "I care very much for you, Peg, but I can't say what you want me to say until I'm sure. That must sound strange, but that's who I am."

Tears stung Peggy's eyes and she turned away from him. "I don't expect you to say anything you don't feel."

Kent grabbed her chin gently and turned her face around, noticing the tears. "Hey, don't do that." He pulled her to him and stroked her hair. "Give me some time, okay? That's all I'm asking."

Peggy held her breath, trying to forestall the sob stuck in her throat. She breathed in and let it out slowly before speaking. "It's all right. I understand." She climbed off his lap and sat opposite him again.

"No, you don't." He maneuvered his wheelchair around the table. "Listen to me…"

"I really don't want to talk about it anymore." She stood up and walked over to the open patio door, blinking back the tears about to spill down her face.

"You want me to be honest with you, don't you? If I said I loved you when I wasn't sure, wouldn't that be worse than not saying it at all?"

She answered without turning around. "I … guess so." The words caught in her throat.

"Peggy, come here. Please."

"I'm kind of tired; it's been quite a day." She headed for the hallway. "I'm going to bed. See you in the morning."

Kent called after her. "Come on, Peg, please don't be like this." He heard the echo of the bedroom door and knew she wasn't coming back. "Dammit!"

Eighteen

Jeff sat at his desk fingering the passport sized photo of Peggy that she had given him for his wallet. Looking at her beautiful, smiling face, he wondered how she was and whether things had worked out the way she'd hoped with Kent. He missed her—missed holding her, the smell of her hair, the feel of her body against his, and as hard as he tried he couldn't get her out of his system. He wanted to—he needed to, but he couldn't. He was in love with her.

His quiet reflection was suddenly interrupted when he realized someone was standing behind him. He turned around.

"Why don't you call her?" the young woman said. "You'll never know what's happening unless you do."

Jeff shook his head. "She made it perfectly clear the last time we spoke that Kent was the man she wanted. There's no hope for me, Kristy."

"If you love her don't give up so easily. She'll realize who the best man is, eventually. If you just leave things the way they are what choice does she have? She's with the man she thinks she's in love with, but is she … or is it infatuation? He is a celebrity, after all. You're real and your feelings for her are real, and she cared for you before she left. What makes you think she still doesn't?"

Jeff gave a thin smile. "How can someone so young be so wise?"

"It doesn't take a science degree to understand love. And, if what you've said is any indication, she still loves you, underneath her attraction for Kent. You should call her."

"I don't know." Jeff slid the photo back into his wallet.

"Think about it. What have you got to lose?" Kristy went back to her desk.

Jeff pondered what she'd said. What did he have to lose? If he fought for Peggy could he win?

His extension buzzed, pulling him out of his contemplation, and he picked up the receiver. It was his editor. "Hi Charlie, what can I do for you?"

"Can you come up to my office? I want to talk to you about something important."

Jeff stood up. "I'm on my way." He dropped the receiver into its cradle and headed to the elevator.

Charlie Lockwood was standing at his office door when Jeff stepped out of the lift. The editor waved for him to hurry up. Jeff picked up his pace and followed Charlie into his office. The older man closed the door behind them. "Take a seat." He gestured to the chair in front of his desk. "So, how are things with you? Did you get that article in?"

"Sure. Why do you ask?" Jeff frowned.

"I just wanted to make sure you had nothing in your calendar right now." Charlie sat down and rummaged through papers on his desk.

"Why is that?" Jeff shifted uneasily in his seat, crossed one leg over the other and folded his arms across his chest.

What was Charlie trying to say? He wasn't getting fired, was he?

"Huh? Because I have a *big* assignment for you." He continued rummaging.

"Oh? Well, why didn't you say so?" Jeff's mood lightened. "What is it?"

"You're okay to travel, right? Passport and all that?"

Jeff eyed his boss with a frown. "Sure. Why, where are you sending me?"

"LA."

"LA?" Jeff's voice raised a decibel. He could hardly believe it.

"Yeah. I want you to cover a breaking story." Charlie found what he was looking for. "Here it is. Can you be ready to leave tomorrow?" He pushed the sheet of paper across the desk.

Jeff picked it up and read the information. "Bloody hell! You want me to cover the story on Kent Reynolds's new lover?"

Unfortunately, he already knew the answer.

Nineteen

Peggy woke up to find she was alone in Kent's huge bed. She glanced across at the bedside clock and gasped. It was almost 11.30. She had never slept in this late before. It had to be Kent. He certainly was *an amazing stress reliever*, she heard Felicity's words echo in her head. She stretched languidly—her body feeling better than it ever had—flung back the covers and got out of bed.

Where was he?

She padded over to the armchair sitting in the corner of the room by the full-length window and plucked her robe off the armrest. She wrapped it around her naked body and tied the belt. The day outside looked glorious. LA's weather was similar to Queensland's, which made her feel more at home. Peggy crossed the room and opened the door. "Kent," she called. All was silent. She wondered if he was out by the pool having a late breakfast. She padded barefoot along the hallway, through the living room and out to the patio. No sign of him.

Could he be taking a shower? She hadn't thought about checking the bathroom. Peggy wandered back through the house, across Kent's room, and into the bathroom. She pushed the door open. No water running. She frowned. Where could he be? He hadn't left a note.

She heard a sound behind her and spun around.

Kent was standing in the doorway without the cast. "Hey." He smiled.

Peggy rushed into his arms. "I was getting worried about you."

"Why? I left a note for you in the kitchen." He slid his arms around her, kissed her forehead, and pulled her to him.

Peggy gazed up at him. "You did? I didn't go into the kitchen. I looked everywhere else, though."

He gave her a cheeky smile. "Want to try out the new me? As we're already in the bathroom, we could take a shower together."

Peggy remembered the dream she'd had at the Versace hotel. The one Kent had wanted to act on. Now he could. "Sure, why not?" She grinned seductively and led him by the hand toward the over-sized shower cubicle. She reached behind the glass and flicked on the tap. Warm water gushed from the shower head and she tugged Kent under the spray, clothes and all.

Kent peeled off his soaking T-shirt and dropped it onto the floor. He pulled Peggy to him and stroked her wet hair. "I realized something today."

"You did?"

"Yeah." He untied the belt on her drenched bathrobe and slid it off her shoulders. It fell into a wet heap at her feet. He trailed kisses across her left shoulder.

"What was that?" Peggy sighed as she unclipped the stud on his jeans and slid the zipper down.

"I love you," he whispered into her ear.

Peggy froze. She gazed up into his beautiful brown eyes, a questioning frown on her face.

"Yes, Peg, you heard right. *I love you.*" He kissed her in that soft, warm, sensual way that made Peggy's insides turn to jelly. She couldn't breathe. Her head swam. *He loved her.*

Kent slid out of his soggy jeans and kicked them off, then lifted her into his arms, carried her across the bedroom, lowered her onto their huge bed and climbed over her. He wasn't ready to make love to her just yet; he wanted to take his time. He eased his body onto hers and sucked one erect nipple into his mouth, teasing the hard pink node with the tip of his tongue. Peggy moaned with pleasure, as the words *'I love you'* drifted into her dazed thoughts. Her body ached for him.

He trailed slow kisses all over her body, down the middle of her stomach, circling his tongue around her belly button, then hovered above that delicate spot. His warm breath on her skin caused the sensitive mound to swell in anticipation. She raised her hips off the bed, eager for Kent to taste her.

He wanted to arouse her senses, and make her want him even more. He kissed a trail down her inner thigh and then traced it back. Peggy moaned in aroused frustration, she lifted her head off the pillow and frowned at him. "What are you doing?"

"Tantalizing your senses. I want to give you an amazing orgasm." He moved his mouth to her other thigh.

"You already do when we make love. Can you just…?"

"Relax and enjoy," he told her. "It'll be worth it, I promise."

She sighed and flopped back onto the pillows.

Kent ran his hand slowly down her thigh and his lips followed the trail with hot, moist kisses. Peggy moaned in expectation of his tongue exploring her. Kent slipped two fingers into her warm wetness while his mouth teased the pulsing core of her womanhood. Her senses soared as Kent's tongue slid around the sensitive nub and his fingers moved rhythmically inside her. It wasn't long before every fiber of her body exploded in an exhilarating rush.

Peggy wanted him now. She playfully wrestled him onto his back and straddled him, taking his hard length inside her. They both moaned with pleasure as their bodies moved in rhythm and gained momentum. Kent massaged her full breasts and teased the nipples with his fingers, heightening her aroused senses. Her breathing quickened, her body tightened. She threw her head back and gave a long pleasurable moan as every nerve ending in her body erupted in pure ecstasy.

Kent wasn't far behind her. His body tensed then shuddered beneath her and his hard length pulsed inside her. Peggy eased herself off him and they lay in each other's arms sated.

Twenty

Jeff arrived at LAX hungry and jetlagged. It was around 1.15 p.m. and after such a long flight, all he wanted to do was get out of the airport and head to the hotel. Getting through security seemed to take hours, and by the time he got to the luggage pick up point it was almost 3.00 p.m.

The paper had organized a rental car, so now all he had to do was get on the shuttle that would take him to the Alamo car rental company and pick it up. As he tugged his over-stuffed suitcase out to the shuttle stop, he wished he wasn't in LA. How could he do a story on Kent and Peggy? What was he supposed to say?

He'd wanted to see her, talk to her, but not like this. This was going to be difficult. And once Peggy knew why he was there, it would be damn near impossible to talk to her without her being furious with him. Would she think this was his way of getting back at her? He hoped she knew him better than that. What had he gotten himself into? Had his feelings for her clouded his judgment that much? Obviously they had.

The shuttle bus arrived, and the driver stepped out to help him with his suitcase. Jeff wanted to turn around and go back home, but he was stuck. He needed to work, and he needed to see Peggy. And he had no choice about either.

It took around ten minutes to get to the car rental company, and once there, Jeff signed the paperwork, hauled his luggage out to the car park and picked up his convertible. You had to drive a convertible in LA. He drove the car out of the lot and headed for Beverly Hills.

He was staying at the Beverly Hilton on Santa Monica Boulevard. It was in a convenient location, handy to everything, and Kent's residence wasn't far from the hotel. The actor owned a house in the Hollywood Hills. Jeff decided to settle into the hotel, take a shower to freshen up, and have a bite to eat before driving by the actor's home.

Kent's home was prestigious indeed, and as Jeff drove by he took in the detail of the double-story mansion. He had his camera with him, but wouldn't take pictures this time round. There was no car in the drive, so they must have been out and about somewhere. He decided to cruise around and see if he could spot Kent's Porsche parked near a restaurant or hotel.

Even though he felt uncomfortable about snapping photos of them, he was in LA to do a job and had a limited amount of time, so he'd just have to shelve his feelings and get on with it. He turned the convertible around and headed to Sunset Boulevard, where most celebs chose to eat and socialize.

The boulevard was buzzing. Shoppers, traffic, and open double-decker tourist buses with people snapping photos as they travelled past the Al Fresco cafés. If celebrities didn't want the attention, why patronize these restaurants and sit outside?

He cruised along one side of the boulevard, then did a U-turn and cruised along the other. When he stopped at the red light he spotted Kent and Peggy leaving one of the restaurants. The light flashed green and Jeff drove through the intersection. They were walking along the street, arm in arm, laughing and talking with another celebrity couple Jeff recognized. The group stopped at Kent's Porsche and said their goodbyes before he opened the door for Peggy and helped her into the car, then moved to the driver's side and got in.

Jeff pulled into a side street not far up the road, and waited for the Porsche to drive past before turning onto the boulevard and tailing them at a reasonable distance. He felt like the paparazzi—intruding on their privacy. And, in all fairness, he was. It seemed Peggy had made her choice and it wasn't him.

He followed the Porsche back to the hills and waited at the end of Kent's street until the car pulled into the driveway, then travelled along the narrow street and pulled into the curb a couple of houses along. Jeff grabbed his camera and got out of the car. He walked back down the street and stopped at the neighboring fence line. Kent was helping Peggy out of the coupe.

He snapped a couple of photos, using the telephoto function on his digital SLR camera to get a closer shot. Kent took Peggy's hand and led her to the double front doors. Jeff did a quick check of the pics then shot a couple more before the pair disappeared into the house. He felt like a peeping Tom and a spurned ex-lover, which, in a way, he was.

Jeff checked the other shots and as he turned to head back to his car he heard a voice call out 'Hey'. He swung around and was confronted by Kent Reynolds strutting down his driveway.

"Can't we get any privacy at all from you guys? You follow us around all day, waiting for that elusive shot. This is my home, man. Don't you have any scruples?" He frowned at Jeff for a moment. "Haven't we met before?"

Jeff was shocked. He hadn't realized he'd been seen, let alone recognized. "Look, I'm sorry Mr. Reynolds. I'm just doing my job."

"I know you." He shoved a finger at Jeff. "You're the guy Peggy went to dinner with back in Australia." He opened the gate and stepped onto the street. "You are … right?"

He'd been caught out. What could he say? "Yes, Mr. Reynolds, I am."

"Then what the hell are you doing? Do you want to embarrass her by pasting her picture all over some gritty tabloid?"

"No. That's not who I'm working for or why I'm…"

Kent waved him off. "Don't bother." He walked back through the gate, shaking his head in disgust.

Jeff rushed to the gates. "Wait a minute. Are you going to tell her?"

The actor turned around, an incredulous look on his face. "What do you think? She has a right to know what kind of douche bag she went out with."

Kent had no idea. He didn't know they had been much

more than just a couple of dates. The thought occurred to Jeff to tell him, but he let it go. Maybe it would be better for Peggy to think he was what she had first thought—a hungry journalist.

Jeff called out to Kent as he walked toward the house. "I'm doing the piece for the Courier Mail, not a gritty tabloid."

Kent turned around. "Does it matter? She thought you were a good guy and now you're selling her out."

Jeff couldn't argue with that.

Twenty one

Peggy was on the phone the minute Kent finished telling her what had happened outside. She couldn't believe Jeff was in LA doing something so appalling. Why would he do that? Then it occurred to Peggy that he wasn't actually doing anything to her, it was Kent he wanted to get at. He was the celebrity.

Jeff answered the call on the second ring, and Peggy didn't give him a chance to speak. "How could you do this? You fly over here without telling me, and then sneak around snapping pictures of us. Are you trying to get back at me for choosing Kent?" She regretted saying it the minute the words left her mouth. She knew he wasn't the kind of man who would do that.

Jeff's heart turned to lead in his chest. He thought she would know that wasn't the reason. "Peggy, if you'll give me a minute to explain…"

"Explain? What could you possibly say that would explain betraying my trust like this?"

"Love, it's not what you think. I wish you would listen for a minute."

Peggy sucked in a deep breath and let it out slowly. She was so angry and hurt her body was trembling, but she realized she needed to hear what he had to say. "All right, I'm listening."

"Thank you." He sighed. "I was offered this assignment, and I took it because I wanted to see you. I really didn't think about the consequences. I'm sorry. But I am a journo, and I do need to eat. You have to know I would never do anything to hurt you."

"How can you say that? You're snapping photos of us to publish."

"Yes, but I'd never let them print anything distasteful. You have to believe that. Will you meet me so we can talk about this? I'd really like to see you."

"Where are you staying? I'll come to you," she said, her voice tight.

Even in this tense moment, Jeff couldn't help smile. At least he'd get to see her again. "I'm at the Hilton hotel on Santa Monica Boulevard."

"I'll be there as soon as I can." Peggy hung up.

Kent paced the living room. "You're going to see him?"

"I have to. I have to make it final."

"What do you mean?"

Peggy took his hand and led him to the sofa. "Sit down. There's something I have to tell you."

He sat down and frowned at her. "What is it?" He had a squirming feeling in the pit of his stomach he wasn't going to like what she was about to say.

"When you left and I didn't hear from you, I assumed you'd gone back home and moved on with your life."

"I know." Kent shifted in his seat and folded his arms across his chest. "So, what are you saying? That you had a thing with this guy?"

Peggy wouldn't look him in the face. Kent stood up, walked over to her and lifted her face up to meet his frowning gaze. "Did you sleep with him?"

Tears welled in her eyes and she nodded.

Kent sighed, pulled her to him and stroked her hair. "It's my fault. I should've made it clear how I felt before I left. How were you to know? And when you didn't hear from me what were you supposed to think?"

Peggy gazed up at him, tears spilling down her face. "I wish I could take it back. I've hurt you both and I never meant to. I don't know what I was thinking."

"I haven't been an angel, either. I hurt you too. We're both guilty of being stupid, if nothing else."

They held each other for a long time, then Peggy eased herself out of Kent's comforting arms. "I'd better go. I said I'd be there soon."

Kent nodded. "Do you want me to drive you?"

Peggy shook her head. "I would really love that, but this is something I have to do by myself." She touched his face. "Thank you, though. I really appreciate the offer."

Jeff was waiting outside the hotel for Peggy to arrive. When she drove in, he watched her pull Kent's Porsche into the curb and waited for her to get out before walking over. He could see she wasn't happy and he was the reason. That didn't sit well with him. He would never intentionally do anything to hurt her. Ever.

Peggy sighed. She just wanted to get the unpleasantness over with. "Hello."

"How are you?" He leaned in to kiss her cheek, but she turned away from him. "Well, that was awkward." He gave a thin smile.

"What did you expect? This hasn't exactly been the ideal reunion, has it?" Peggy passed him and headed for the front entrance.

"Can I buy you a cup of coffee? We can find a quiet corner and talk." He caught up to her and took her by the arm, leading her into the lobby.

"All right. But I can't stay long."

"I see." He frowned at her. "Kent waiting for you to hurry back, is he?"

"Jeff." She glowered at him sideways.

"Sorry, but I'd like to try to sort this out. I'd like to remain friends, if that's at all possible?"

Peggy didn't answer.

They entered the hotel, walked over to the café and found a quiet spot near the grand piano.

Jeff pulled a chair out for Peggy and she sat down.

"Can I get you anything?" He asked.

"Yes, thanks. A low-fat decaf latte."

Jeff ordered the drinks then came back and sat opposite Peggy, watching her for a moment.

He started to say something, but Peggy cut him off.

"Before you say anything, I want to say something."

He looked at her with a questioning frown.

"I want to tell you how sorry I am for everything that's happened between us. I never meant to hurt you. But I can't help the way I feel. I thought I could hide my feelings from myself, but I realized I couldn't. I hope you can understand that."

Jeff hadn't expected an apology. He'd expected to be berated for being an intruder in her new life with Kent. "Well, I appreciate that, I really do, love. I guess I knew what I was getting myself into and that you still had unresolved feelings for Kent, but I was willing to take that chance in the hope that, perhaps, you could fall in love with me." He sighed. "I was fooling myself. Deep down I knew that." He patted her hand.

Peggy gazed across the table at him. She was sorry she'd given him false hope. She'd even fooled herself into thinking she could change how she felt about Kent. But it didn't matter now. It was all out in the open. Her thoughts returned to the photos.

"What are you going to do…?" She was interrupted by the waitress with their order. Peggy waited until she was gone. "As I was about to say, what are you going to do about the photos? You can't be serious about publishing them."

Jeff poured milk into his tea and looked at her. "What else can I do? I'm here on assignment. I can't go back empty handed, can I?"

She frowned. "And you can't print those photos."

"Love, you've been out in public. If I've seen you, so has everyone else. It's going to be common knowledge soon enough." He stirred two teaspoons of sugar into his tea.

Peggy pondered what he'd said for a moment. "That may be true, but…"

"But what? If I saw you on Sunset Boulevard, members of the paparazzi did too. We're probably having this

155

argument needlessly. Someone else may already be printing similar photos of you as we speak."

The reality of his words brought home the fact that she was angry about the whole situation: hurting him, hurting Kent, and running off to LA … all of it. It really had nothing to do with the photos. "All right." She sipped her Latte.

"All right what?"

"You're right." She frowned at him. "I give up."

"I don't want you to give up." He reached across and touched her hand. "I want you to be happy. That's all I've ever wanted."

"And what about you? Are you going to be happy?" She looked at him, knowing he wasn't.

"Not right now, no. But I will be." He gave her a thin smile and studied her face for a minute before speaking again. "Can we please call a truce."

Twenty two

Jeff waited in the international departure lounge for his flight back to Australia. His emotions were a mixture of gladness and regret. He was happy he and Peggy had resolved their differences, but sad because he wasn't the man she had chosen.

It was 8.15 p.m. and dark outside. He gazed out of the airport window and sighed. All he could see was his grim reflection staring back at him. He was going to miss Peggy for a long time to come. Jeff remembered the passport-sized photo of her he had in his wallet. He pulled it out of his pants pocket, flipped it open and slid the tiny picture out of the clear plastic sleeve. He sighed as he gazed at her lovely smiling face. It wasn't going to be easy getting over her, but he had to he had no choice. He returned the photo to his wallet and pushed it back into his pocket.

An announcement echoed over the PA system that the flight would board in fifteen minutes. Jeff picked up his bag and walked over to the check in counter, joining the other passengers waiting in line.

As airport staff arrived to prepare for check in, and more people stood up to join the queue, Jeff thought he heard someone call his name. He glanced around the departure lounge, but didn't recognize anyone. He moved forward in the line. Passengers were moving through quickly, he was only a couple of people away from the check in desk.

"Jeff, wait!"

Jeff turned his head and saw Peggy running along the lounge. He stepped out of the queue and rushed toward her. He was elated that she had made a last minute dash to see him off. He smiled. "What are you doing here? I thought we'd already said our goodbyes."

She stopped, puffing. "I couldn't let you leave without seeing you off. What kind of friend would I be?" Peggy wrapped her arms around him and held him for a moment without speaking.

Jeff eased her away from him and looked into her eyes, frowning. "What is it, love?"

She shook her head, but didn't answer. Tears welled in her eyes and she looked away.

He sighed, and lifted her face up to look at him. "What's going on?"

"We've been through so much together in such a short time." She paused for a moment and then said, "I'm truly sorry for everything. I hope you can forgive me."

Jeff pulled her to him. He didn't need this right now, his heart was already aching. As he stroked her hair and gazed along the lounge, he saw Kent waiting in the distance watching them, arms folded across his chest. He eased Peggy out of his embrace. "You'd better go, love. I have to get on the plane."

Peggy gazed across the lounge. Everyone else had boarded and the check in staff were waiting for Jeff. She looked up at him. "All right." She sniffled, holding back more tears. "Look after yourself, won't you?" She tried to smile and look genuinely happy, but it was difficult. "Have a safe flight."

Jeff smiled. "I will. Take care, love." He brushed her cheek with his fingertips then turned and walked away, realizing that although he didn't want to he had to let her go.

Peggy turned and walked back along the lounge to Kent, knowing in her heart she would never see Jeff again. When she reached him, he pulled her into his arms. "Are you all right?"

She looked up into his concerned eyes. "Yes, I'm fine. Saying goodbye is never easy. But it was something I had to do, for closure."

He stroked her hair. "I know."

"Thank you for understanding. You don't know how much it means to me."

Kent eased her away from him. "I think I do." He gave a slight smile. "Why don't we go home?" He took her hand and led her along the empty departure lounge to the security check point. When they reached the door a security officer stepped out to meet them.

"Everything all right?" he asked Kent. "Did you make it in time?"

"Yeah, we did. Thanks, Rick, I appreciate it." Kent shook his hand.

"No problem. Just don't make a habit of it." He smiled.

"I don't plan to."

The officer led the couple through the doors and escorted them out to Kent's car.

Peggy was quiet on the drive back to Kent's mansion. She sat gazing out the passenger window at the car headlights and concrete walls zipping past. She sighed and brushed a single tear from her cheek.

Kent reached across and rested his hand on her thigh. "Hey, honey, you're awfully quiet over there. Are you sure everything's all right?"

She jumped at his touch and swung her head around. "Mm? Sorry. What did you say?"

"Everything all right?" he asked again, a frown of concern on his face.

Peggy gave a thin smile. "Of course. Everything's fine."

Kent took an exit ramp, pulled off the road and turned off the engine. He unclipped his seatbelt and leaned across to her. "What's wrong, Peg?" He reached up and touched her cheek.

She sighed, but didn't answer.

"And before you say 'nothing's wrong', try being honest with me. Do you miss Jeff?"

She frowned at him. "Of course I do. But that's not what I was thinking about."

"What then?" He unclipped her seatbelt and pulled her to him, slipping an arm around her shoulders.

"I was thinking about home and what I was going to do next."

"I hope you're thinking about going home, finalizing everything and coming back to LA. To me."

Peggy looked into his eyes. "You really want me to?"

"What kind of question is that? Of course I do. I want to…"

"You want to what?" She frowned at him.

Kent didn't answer. He gazed into her eyes for a moment then said, "This wasn't how I'd pictured it in my head." He took both her hands in his. "Peggy Anton, would you do me the honor of becoming my wife?" Kent flicked on the interior light, leaned across to the glove compartment and extracted a tiny, dark blue box. "I had hoped to do this over dinner tonight, but here we are." He flipped open the lid and pushed the box toward her. In the center of blue satin sat the most beautiful, diamond engagement ring Peggy had ever seen—a large, solitary, square stone set in a yellow, filigree gold band.

Peggy's mouth gaped. She gazed at the ring and then at Kent. She hadn't expected anything like this.

"I want you with me. And I know you won't settle for anything less than total commitment. So will you..." He plucked the ring from the box, lifted Peggy's left hand and slid the glittering jewel onto her finger. "...marry me?"

Peggy gazed at the ring. It was far too ostentatious, but she wasn't about to spoil the moment. She looked into Kent's questioning eyes and smiled. "Yes, Kent, I would love to be your wife."

Kent pulled her face to him and kissed her in that warm, slow, sensual way that made her insides turn to liquid. He took her breath away.

As her dizzy thoughts became clear, she realized she was going to become Mrs. Kent Reynolds.

Twenty three

Being back in her home felt wrong to Peggy, she'd been away for so long, everything about it seemed alien. She wandered into her bedroom and felt a pang of longing for Kent. She wondered how the movie shoot was going and how long he'd be in New York. She hoped he'd be in LA by the time she got back. She missed him so much already.

Peggy gave a heavy sigh and plonked herself down onto her bed. It was tiny in comparison to the one they shared in Kent's home. She ran her hand over the bedspread and closed her eyes trying to envision Kent lying beside her. She imagined his handsome face smiling back at her and pulled a pillow close and hugged it tight. She would be glad when everything was organized and she was on her way home … to him.

She had been back in Brisbane for three days, had seen Gary to tell him the good news and hand in her resignation. Her boss had been shocked at first, after everything that had happened between Peggy and the actor, but once he was over the initial surprise, told her he was happy for her and hoped everything worked out for them. She insisted that he fly over for the wedding, and Gary promised he would try. She planned to organize an airline ticket for him, once the date was set.

Peggy had arranged money transfers and organized the cancelation of her utilities. All that was left to do was to pack what she wanted to send, and sell the rest. The removal company had delivered enough boxes for her to pack up the house, and she had already packed five. She realized she would have to get serious about what she wanted to keep otherwise she'd end up taking everything.

She opened her eyes, gazed at the ceiling and sighed. Remembering that she and Jeff had spent their last night together making love in her bed, Peggy sat up and pushed the pillow into place, shook her head and stood up. She didn't want to think about Jeff. She strutted out of her room and headed to the kitchen to make a cup of tea. She needed to keep focused or she'd never be ready in time.

The musical tone of her cordless phone broke the silence and Peggy jumped. She laughed at her reaction, rushed over to the phone and snatched it off the wall. "Hello?"

"Hey, honey, how's everything going?" Kent sounded cheerful. "I miss you."

"I miss you, too." A smile spread across her face. Her heart was beating just that little bit faster. Kent always had that effect on her. "Things are going ok. Slower than I'd like, but I'm getting there. How's the movie shoot going?"

"We've had a bit of a hiccup on set. One of the stunt guys got injured today, so I'm in training."

"They can't get another stunt man?" Peggy was worried about Kent being injured too.

"They could, but I want to do them myself. It'll be a good experience for me. More and more actors are doing that now, and the fans love the idea of their favorite celebs doing their own stunts."

"Please be careful. I don't want you hurt. If a professional can get injured, so can you." She could hear the panic in her voice. "We've already been through that once, remember."

"Hey, don't worry. I'll be fine. They take every precaution. There's nothing to worry about, I promise."

Peggy didn't answer.

"Peggy?" His tone was firm.

"Yes?"

His voice softened. "Please don't worry about me. I'll be ok."

"I'll take your word for it, but I can't promise not to worry. I love you." Peggy tried to conceal the concern in her voice.

"I love you too. I'd better go, it's getting late and we still have a scene to shoot. I'll call you tomorrow."

"All right. I'll talk to you then." Kent rang off, and Peggy slid the phone onto the kitchen counter. She would worry about him. How could she not?

The attractive young actress knocked on Kent's trailer door and waited for it to swing open. She was dressed in a low-cut, red, off the shoulder top and short denim skirt. She'd managed to get her hands on a bottle of champagne and two plastic cups and thought she'd share her find with the actor. Why not? They could make a night of it. Kent Reynolds had a reputation for being a master in the bedroom and she wanted to experience his talents firsthand.

Kent opened the door and was surprised to see the young woman standing at the bottom of the steps. It was a few minutes after 2.00 a.m. He'd been sitting in bed going over his lines for the next day, and was wearing nothing more than a luxurious, cotton bath robe.

"Hi, Courtney, isn't it past your bedtime?" he said with indifference. She was probably no more than twenty, less than half his age. Not that it had bothered him before, but it did now.

She held up the champagne bottle. "I found this and thought I'd share." She gave him a seductive smile. "Aren't you going to invite me in?"

Kent pursed his lips and considered his options. Should he? One drink couldn't hurt. He held up his index finger. "One drink and then it's bedtime."

Courtney giggled. "That's what I was hoping for." She climbed the three metal steps and squeezed past Kent, brushing herself against him deliberately.

He ran his gaze over her curvaceous body as he pulled the door to and followed her over to the sofa. She positioned herself in the center, crossing one long, tanned leg over the other, and passed him the bottle. "Would you mind opening this for me?" She smiled again, batting her long lashes at him.

Kent slid the bottle from her hand and walked over to the kitchen counter. Within seconds, he'd uncorked it without the loud pop and poured champagne into two crystal glasses.

Courtney glanced at the white plastic cups in her hand and pushed them onto the lamp table beside the sofa. Kent held the champagne out to her. "Thanks," she said, taking the elegant, long-stemmed glass from his hand, their fingers touching. She raised the glass for a toast. "To an entertaining evening." She clinked her glass against his and took a sip.

Kent eased himself into an armchair opposite her, but didn't drink the champagne. Instead, he set the glass down on the small table between the chairs, folded his arms across his chest and studied her. She was quite attractive. Long, white blond hair pulled back in a ponytail, tanned complexion, exotic eyes and sumptuous mouth. The top she was wearing didn't leave much to the imagination; her breasts must have been at least a size double something—probably fake. Neither did the short denim skirt, which had revealed the cheeks of her firm behind just below the hemline when she'd strutted past him. It would have been a turn on once, and he would have been eager to get her into bed, but not now.

Courtney swallowed the last of her champagne, and held her glass out for more. Kent got up, walked to the counter, picked up the bottle and poured more champagne into her glass. She took another sip, sat the slender glass on the table, stood up and gazed into Kent's attractive brown eyes.

"You're not drinking," she said with a pout, noticing his untouched glass. "Don't you like champagne?" She reached up and curled some stray strands of his hair around her fingers.

"It's a bit late for me." He stepped away from her, sitting the half empty bottle on the counter behind him.

She was offended. "What's wrong, Kent, don't you like me?" She stepped closer, pushing one hand inside his robe to rub his smooth muscular chest.

Kent grabbed her by the wrist. "Don't do that." He pushed her hand away.

"Why not? Don't you want to?"

"Courtney, you're a lovely young lady but…"

The young woman flung herself at him, reaching under his robe and probing places she shouldn't be touching. Kent pushed her away. "I said don't. What part of *don't* don't you understand?"

She pressed herself against him like an affectionate cat, rubbing her breasts against his chest. "Come on, Kent, I'm giving myself to you. Take me, I want you to." She ran her hands all over his robe, and then attempted to untie the belt. She looked up at him and smiled. "I know what you want," she said, lowering herself onto her knees and sliding her tongue across her glossy pink lips.

Kent sighed. "Courtney, stop." He took her by the arm and pulled her up off the floor. "I said *no*." He eased her backward and sat her down on the sofa.

Courtney gazed up at him, tears welling in hers. "Why don't you want me?" Her pouty lower lip quivered. "I'm not pretty enough for you, is that it?"

"No, that's not it. I have someone in my life now. Someone very important to me and I don't want to do anything to screw it up."

"But I heard you'll sleep with someone even if you are dating. I won't tell anyone we did it. I promise."

"That was the old me. I don't do that anymore." He walked over to the door and swung it open. "Time to go, Courtney. It's late."

Twenty four

Peggy had finalized her affairs within a few days and said her goodbyes to family and friends. Her belongings would be on their way to LA the next afternoon, and so would she in a matter of a few hours. She'd made a hotel reservation in Brisbane city for her last night in Australia, and was on her way to check in when her cell phone rang. She plucked it from her bag. It was Kent.

She was in the back of a cab only minutes from the hotel. "Hi, I didn't expect a call tonight. Is everything ok?"

"Are you at the hotel?"

"No, I'm in a cab. It shouldn't take more than five or ten minutes. Why?" Her stomach knotted. She could hear the tension in his voice and knew something was wrong.

"I'll call you back when you've checked in."

Peggy dropped her phone into her bag and frowned. Kent sounded stressed and she wondered what was on his mind. Could he have had a change of heart? Peggy was worried.

Check in took only a few minutes as most of the information had been provided when she'd made the reservation. Peggy was eager to get up to her room and wait for Kent's call. Her luggage had already been taken up. She crossed the lobby and waited for the elevator, her nerves on edge. Kent's tense tone bothered her. What did he want to talk to her about?

Peggy entered the room, walked over to the luxurious queen-size bed and sat down. She reached into her bag, pulled out her phone and stared at the screen, willing Kent to call back. Her stomach churned. Something was wrong, she could feel it.

The phone went off, vibrating in her hand to the tune of *Africa,* by Toto, and she almost dropped it. "Hello, what's going on?"

"Hi, honey, something's happened. I want you to listen to what I have to say without interruption and without jumping to conclusions. Can you please do that?"

Peggy was silent for a moment, then she answered, "I can try. What's happened?"

He gave a heavy sigh. "A photo appeared in…"

"Oh, no, did Jeff finally publish those photos he took of us?"

"Honey, please, just listen. This has nothing to do with Jeff." He ran a hand through his hair and then over his face. "One of the young actresses visited me in my trailer. It was early in the morning and because my lights were on, I guess she decided to knock. She brought champagne with her and wanted to share it. I told her one glass and then she'd have to go. She finished her glass of champagne and then started to…"

"Did you sleep with her?"

Kent couldn't believe she was asking him that.

"*No.* Will you hear me out before jumping to the *wrong* conclusion?" He could hear her sigh on the other end of the phone. "Please, Peg?"

"I'm listening."

"She wanted more, but I told her I was with someone and I didn't do that kind of thing anymore. The whole stupid incident lasted less than ten minutes, then I asked her to go. I guess that's when the sleaze ball photographer got the pic of her leaving. Who'd have guessed someone would be hanging around at that time of night just waiting for a shot? Maybe he'd followed her and knew it was my trailer, I don't know."

Peggy's heart ached. Kent had gone back to his old philandering ways while she'd been away. "Don't you mean it's unfortunate you got caught?" Tears stung her eyes and spilled down her face. "How could you do this to me, Kent? You just asked me to marry you. If you didn't want to get married…"

"I've done *nothing* wrong. Why won't you believe that? I love you. I'm *in love* with you. And that's something I've never said to any woman—ever! Why would I do that to us?"

"Maybe because you're a selfish bastard who only thinks about himself." She was furious with him.

Kent was angry that she didn't trust him. "I haven't done anything to deserve this from you. Have I slept with anyone other than you since we've been together?"

"How should I know? You're gone for hours…"

"Don't go there, Peg. I've been totally faithful. I don't understand why I have to defend myself to you. I thought of all people you'd believe in me."

Peggy's response was almost inaudible. "I wish I could. But with your previous track record what am I supposed to think?"

Kent paced in his trailer. "I would *never* do that to us. Why can't you believe that?"

Peggy noticed some papers and magazines lying on the bureau under the window. She jumped up off the bed and rushed over to them. Hotels often had tabloids and other magazines in the rooms. She skimmed through them, instantly stopping at an OK magazine. Staring her in the face was a photo of a young blonde leaving Kent's trailer, dressed in skimpy clothes, with him standing at the door barefoot and wearing a bath robe. Peggy raised a hand to her mouth and gasped. "Oh, Kent."

"What is it?" he asked, anxious.

Peggy picked up the magazine, wandered back to the bed, sat down and laid it on the bedspread. She opened to the headline story, *'Kent Reynolds's Late Night Rendezvous with Young Co-star'*, and was horrified to see a series of photos—the attractive young blonde, with shoes in hand, kissing Kent goodbye. And another photo of her waving and blowing kisses at him as she left.

"Are you there?" Kent asked.

"I have the magazine."

"Honey, please believe me, it's *not* what it looks like."

Peggy stared at the glossy pictures. "How can you say that when the proof is right in front of me?"

"What I told you is the truth. I *did not* sleep with her!"

"You're standing at the door in a robe. What were you wearing underneath?"

"You've been with me long enough to know that I was naked. I'd taken a shower and…"

"Before or after you had sex with her?"

"That's not fair."

"I really don't want to talk about it anymore. I won't be flying out tomorrow. I'm going home. Please don't try to contact me. I'll return the ring." She held back the sob burning in her throat.

"Please don't do this. I don't want to lose you.

"Maybe you should've thought about that before having one last fling. Goodbye, Kent." She rang off and burst into tears.

"Shit!" Kent tossed the phone across the room. It hit the wall, smashed and fell to the floor in pieces. He didn't care. He paced the length of his trailer, wondering how he could have been so stupid. How could he have put himself in such a provocative position? The paparazzi had been all over the movie, what made him think they wouldn't stoop so low as to hang outside his trailer in the middle of the night? He should have known, should have been prepared, should have *never* let Courtney into his trailer.

He stopped and gazed at Peggy's picture sitting on the counter. If she loved him she should have believed him, should have trusted him. Why had she been so quick to judge him? Why had she believed the lies in that magazine? Why hadn't she given him the benefit of the doubt? He reached across, picked up the photo and stared at her smiling face. "Why didn't you believe me?"

It had taken him quite some time to translate his true feelings for Peggy, but once he had, he knew he was in love with her and wanted her to be his wife. But now, as he thought about her betrayal, he wasn't sure. If she couldn't trust him—if every time he was away on a movie set she thought he was sleeping with his co-star—what would be the point? He had given her his heart and she had ripped it from his chest.

Kent decided he would not run after her. If she wanted him she'd have to come back to LA and apologize for believing he'd betrayed her. He slid the photo face down onto the counter. "To hell with it. It's the first and last time I try doing the right thing. From now on, I'm living the life I was meant to live. Play the field with *no* strings attached!"

Twenty five

Peggy stood at her kitchen sink, gazing out at her back garden, a mug of tea cooling in front of her. She had spent the night at the Brisbane hotel—only because it had been paid for and there was a no refund policy—and arrived home early this morning to organize having her things returned as soon as possible. Her sister, Iris, would arrive at any minute to help her with the unpacking and setting up. She was grateful. Peggy loved her sister, and it would be nice to spend some time together, even if it was to set up her home again.

The doorbell broke her train of thought and she headed to the front door. She hoped it was Iris and not the removal company.

"Hey, sis, thanks for coming." Peggy hugged her.

"Hey, yourself. It'll be nice to spend some time together. We're both so busy these days we don't do this often enough." Iris stepped inside and closed the door. "So, where do you want to start?"

Peggy headed back to the kitchen, her sister right behind her. "Nowhere at the moment, the removal van hasn't arrived yet."

Iris checked her watch. "What time were they meant to be here?"

Peggy glanced at the kitchen clock, it was 9.50 a.m. "They should be here soon. I asked them to deliver my things around ten. I was lucky they hadn't already gone to the airport."

"Do you want to start with the bedroom so you'll have somewhere to sleep, at least?" Iris dropped her bag onto the kitchen sink, wandered over to the kettle and made herself a mug of coffee.

"Good idea. I really don't feel like camping out in the living room tonight." She gave a thin smile.

The doorbell rang.

"That'll be them."

Iris set her mug down and followed Peggy to the door.

Once all of her things had been brought in, the two women got to work setting up house. As she worked, Peggy couldn't help but think about how different things had turned out. She thought by now she would be landing in LA, and thinking about planning her wedding day. Her heart ached as tears stung her eyes, and she tried to push the thought from her mind.

Iris noticed her sister's unhappy expression and moved around the bed to hug her. "Hey, don't let it get you down. I know it's difficult, but you made the right decision. No one deserves to be cheated on."

"You're right, I know, but why do I feel so bad? Maybe I did jump to conclusions. I do have a habit of doing that. Maybe he was telling the truth."

Iris leaned back and looked into her sister's eyes. "And maybe pigs can fly." She hugged Peggy again. "You deserve better than some self-absorbed, cheating actor."

175

Peggy eased herself out of her sister's arms, suddenly thinking of Jeff. "I did have better, and I ruined it."

"Jeff, you mean?"

"Yes. I should never have let him go. He was so kind and loving. He would never have done this to me. I know that."

"Why don't you call him?"

Peggy shook her head. "I couldn't do that. I hurt him so much. And even though he forgave me…"

"If he loved you, he'd be happy to hear from you."

"I know you mean well, sis, but I can't play with his emotions. He's moved on. It wouldn't be fair."

"What about as friends then?"

Peggy glanced at her sister. "I ... don't know. He was meant to leave for the UK, I don't even know if he's still in the country."

Iris crossed the room, picked up the cordless phone and brought it to her. "Why don't you call him and find out?"

Peggy took the phone from her sister's hand and stared at it. It had been a while since she'd spoken to him, remembering their strained goodbye at LAX. She didn't want him to think she was contacting him to start over again. She wasn't even sure if she should try, not after everything that happened between them.

Iris nudged her sister back to reality. "Hey, what's going through your mind?"

Peggy looked at her. "I don't think I should. What if he's met someone?"

"Do you think he would have moved on so quickly?' Iris rested a comforting hand on Peggy's arm.

"I guess not."

Iris pointed to the phone in her sister's hand. "Go on, call him."

Peggy shook her head and passed the phone back. "I don't need any more complications in my life right now, and neither does he. It wouldn't be fair to either of us. What I do need is some alone time, somewhere peaceful to sort out my feelings. I wish I had the money to holiday on a tropical island or in the mountains."

"Why don't you drive down to Byron Bay? You love it there by the water, and it's away from everything and everyone." Iris owned a vacation house there.

Peggy gazed at her sister wide-eyed. "Really? Are you sure?"

Iris set the phone down and hugged her sister. "Of course I'm sure. We won't be going down there for a month or so, not until the next school holidays. Your suitcases are still packed, so why not stay down there for a while?" Iris went to the kitchen, then returned to her sister's bedroom. "Here." She dropped the keys into Peggy's hand. "The place is all yours, at least for the next few weeks. I'll sort things out here for you while you're gone."

Twenty six

The cocktail party seemed insignificant to Kent, and so did the girl attached to his arm, as he stood *not* listening to the producer in front of him talking about an upcoming movie he'd like the actor to star in. He missed Peggy, and no matter how hard he tried to push his feelings for her into the background and get on with his previous life, they kept resurfacing. And they hurt like hell. He swallowed the last of his champagne, slid the glass onto a tray as a waiter whisked past, unhinged the attractive, but obtuse young woman from the escort agency off his arm and strutted toward the door.

He had to get the love of his life back. And now that he finally admitted it to himself, he had no intention of losing her. He had to do something about it now, no matter what it took. He'd have his manager speak to the director as soon as possible the next morning and tell him they'd have to shoot scenes around him until he got back. If not, he would breach his contract and his lawyers could deal with the fallout.

Two days later he was standing in the First Class departure lounge at LAX, waiting to board a flight to

Australia. The direct flight would take around fourteen hours. It was a flight he had to take. And he had no doubt in his mind that when he returned to LA, Peggy would be with him.

At 3.25 p.m. the following afternoon, Kent arrived at the Brisbane International Airport. He'd arranged a hire car and once he picked it up, he loaded his luggage into the trunk and sped out of the airport parking lot.

Kent turned on the Navman, but wasn't sure how to program it. He pulled into the breakdown lane on Airport Drive, leaving the engine running, and fiddled with the navigation device. After several minutes of fumbling, he managed to get it to work. He keyed in Peggy's address, then pulled out onto the road and continued his drive down to the coast at the direction of the composed, computerized, American female voice.

The drive along the Pacific Highway was pleasant and flowed well. Kent had hired a silver, BMW convertible and had the top down. The cloudless sky was blue, the sun radiant, and it was a glorious Queensland afternoon. He'd been recognized a few times by people driving past. They beeped their horns, waved and smiled. He waved and smiled back. One passenger pulled out a cell phone and snapped a couple of pictures. Kent didn't mind it went with the territory, and he had more important things to think about.

His stomach tightened as he took the exit ramp off the highway. He wasn't far from Peggy's home. What would she say when she saw him? What could he say to her to get her to change her mind?

Kent pulled off the road for a moment, his stomach tight, his doubts getting the better of him. Peggy had sent the engagement ring back by international registered mail. What if she never wanted to see him again? *No, that won't happen. I won't let that happen.*

He eased the convertible back onto the road and drove another kilometer before turning into Peggy's street. Kent cruised along, checking the numbers, and pulled up opposite her cottage-style home. "So, this is where you live," he said, smiling at the modest house that suited her perfectly. He turned off the engine and sat for a minute, before pulling the keys from the ignition and getting out of the car. He pressed the button to set the immobilizer and crossed the street.

Kent walked up the path to the front door and felt the knot of apprehension tighten even more in his stomach. He had never felt like this about anyone before. Peggy was *the one* and he had no intention of letting her go.

He stepped onto the front porch and stared at the deep red door with a brass lion's head knocker. He raised his hand to grip the knocker but pulled back, his palm sweaty. He swallowed the nervous lump in his throat—he could do this, he had to—and knocked on the door.

"Just a minute," someone call from inside. It wasn't Peggy. The door swung open. "Can I help you?" the woman asked, offering him a curious frown.

"I hope so. I'm looking for Peggy Anton. She does live here, doesn't she?"

The woman, who Kent thought resembled Peggy, frowned. "Are you a friend of hers?"

Perhaps Peggy hadn't told her about him. Or maybe she was being aloof because she knew about the breakup.

"Ah, yes, I am. Is she here?"

"No. She's ... away. She won't be back for a few days." She knew who he was, but wasn't about to give him any information about her sister's whereabouts. "Would you like to leave a message? I'll make sure she gets it."

"It's very important that I see her. Can you to tell me where she is?"

The woman shook her head and grimaced. "Sorry."

"Okay. When will she be back?"

She hesitated for a moment. Should she tell him? "Saturday. Can I let her know you stopped by? If you want to leave a name and number..."

"I'll come back when she's here. Thanks for your time." Kent sighed and walked down the path. He could feel the woman's gaze still on him. When he reached the gate, he turned and waved. "Thanks again."

He crossed the street and got into the car. What was he going to do now? Where could she be? The woman had given nothing away.

Kent headed to the Versace hotel. It was close by and jet lag had begun to set in. He'd decide what to do after a good night's sleep.

After checking into the hotel and being escorted to his suite, Kent showered, changed into a fresh pair of boxers and fell into bed. He was exhausted physically, mentally and emotionally. When he closed his eyes, Peggy's smiling face appeared in his head. Kent pulled a spare pillow to him and hugged it tight, missing her and wishing she was here wrapped in his arms as he drifted off to sleep.

Twenty seven

Peggy sat on the sand watching the white foamy waves ebbing in and out, depositing stringy clumps of seaweed along the shore line. The balmy breeze and gentle rush of the sea were soothing to her senses. She had been at the seaside cottage for four weeks, and the time away had revitalized her soul. She was looking forward to getting back to her ordinary life, where people were real. She didn't belong in Tinseltown. She wasn't superficial, hungry for money, or glamorous enough. But, as she sat and gazed at the water rippling across the sand, she realized that Kent was hovering in the back of her thoughts, and she wondered if her heart would ever be free of him.

She gave a heavy sigh, knowing she had to get him out of her system once and for all. It was over, nothing would change that. Peggy climbed to her feet, picked up her sandals and her towel and shook out the sand. It was time to put it all behind her and move on with her life. When she turned around to begin her walk back, she was surprised to see Jeff standing in the shade of the bordering trees.

Iris must have contacted him. Peggy wished she hadn't. She trudged the warm sand, and when she got closer he gave her a brief wave and a smile.

"Hi, love, how are you?" he said as she stepped into the shade.

"I'm good. You?" She could hear the tension in her voice.

"Better for seeing you." His smile widened.

Peggy gave a thin smile, feeling awkward. "It's good to see you, too."

"Is it? Come here then." He reached out and pulled her to him.

Peggy didn't resist, she let herself be drawn against his firm, masculine body. It felt good to be wrapped in safe, strong arms, and she slid her arms around him, tears threatening to spill. They stood together for a long time holding each other. Silent. Letting the feelings they once had for one another envelop them.

They sat across the kitchen table in uncomfortable silence, looking at the untouched cups of tea cooling in front of them. It had been a couple of months since they'd seen each other. The last time at LAX, when Jeff was traveling back to Australia.

Peggy was the first to speak. "How have you been?"

Jeff glanced over at her, his eyes betraying his emotions. "I've missed you."

She shifted uncomfortably on her chair, picked up her cup of tepid tea and sipped it. "I'm sorry, Jeff, but…"

"I know. You're still in love with him despite everything he's done to you."

Peggy set her cup on its saucer and frowned at him. "We were engaged to be married. I can't just turn my feelings off." Although she wished she could.

Jeff reached across the table and touched her hand. She didn't pull away. "I'm sorry he hurt you, love."

She tried to smile, but there was still so much pain inside. "It's not your fault. Why should you be sorry?"

He stood up, moved around the table and held out his arms. "Come here."

Peggy hesitated for a moment, then stood up and walked into Jeff's comforting embrace.

"Is there anything I can do?"

She glanced up at him. "Not really. I need to work this out on my own. Iris shouldn't have called you. I asked her not to."

"Why?" He eased her away from him and frowned.

Peggy stepped back and sat down. "Because it's not fair to you."

The corner of his mouth went up in a half smile. "I'm a big boy, love, I can take care of myself. Don't worry about me." He moved back to his chair.

She sighed. "I know you can. I just don't want you to think there's any hope of…"

"I won't. I'm here because you need a friend." He reached across the table and took her hand. "I can't turn my feelings off either, but I'm not about to let them get in the way of being here for you."

Peggy gazed into his sincere eyes and felt a pang of guilt, and regret. Had she made the wrong choice? Could Jeff be the man she was meant to be with? How could he sit there holding her hand, wanting to help, and not be hurt? She sighed. Men were so hard to figure out sometimes. That was an understatement where Kent was concerned.

"When were you planning to head back home?" Jeff asked.

"In the morning. I was going to stay until Saturday but I need to get back. I don't even know if I'll have a job to go back to."

"Would you mind if I stayed and drove back with you? I've got a rental I can drop off in town. We can do that in the morning before we leave, if that's all right?"

Peggy frowned at him and hesitated before answering. It would be awkward having him stay the night, but she couldn't say no after him coming all this way to help her.

Twenty eight

K ent ate breakfast in his hotel suite, then called the Sofitel in Brisbane to cancel his reservation. It would be far more convenient for him to stay at the Versace as it was only about twenty minutes from Peggy's home, and he wanted to be within close proximity.

She would be back on Saturday and he wanted to be at her front door bright and early Sunday morning with an enormous bunch of dusky pink Gerberas ready to tell her how much she meant to him and how much he wanted her to be his wife.

He'd made up his mind that he was *not* going back to Los Angeles without her. Peggy was the woman he loved and wanted to spend the rest of his life with—there was no question about that now—and he wasn't going to give up until she took him back, no matter how long it took. He'd wait it out.

In the meantime, Kent planned to keep a low profile. Nothing would jeopardize his reunion with her. No paparazzi, no besotted starlet, no sleazy tabloid story, *nothing!* He picked up the remote control, turned on the flat screen television, plumped his pillows and settled back. It was going to be a long, boring couple of days, but he would endure it for her. He sighed and channel surfed, hoping there was something watchable on the box.

Twenty nine

I ris's eyes lit up when she opened the door and saw Peggy and Jeff standing on the porch. She swung the door back and gave her sister a tight hug. "Hi, how was the cottage?"

"Lovely. It was just what I needed. The beach and the quiet was very therapeutic." Peggy stepped inside and Jeff followed her in, carrying the bags.

"I'm glad." Iris closed the door and joined them in the living room.

"I feel refreshed." Peggy sat down on the sofa.

Jeff put the bags in her room, then joined the ladies in the living room, sitting next to Peggy.

"Did you manage to get things sorted out in your mind about what you're going to do?" Iris sat in an armchair opposite them.

Peggy frowned. "I know I have to get on with my life, but it's not going to be that easy. I can't just turn my feelings off. I wish I could, believe me."

Jeff reached across and squeezed her hand. She eased her hand out of his, feeling self-conscious in front of her sister.

Iris had a worried frown on her face, and Peggy noticed.

"What's wrong?" she asked, seeing her sister's expression change.

"Nothing. It's nothing." Iris shook her head.

"Come on, sis, spit it out. Something's bothering you. What is it?"

Iris sighed. "While you were away someone came to see you."

Peggy moved forward on her seat. "Who?"

Iris clasped her hands in her lap. "Ah … him."

"Him?" Peggy raised a hand to her forehead. "Kent you mean? He was here? When?"

"A couple of days ago. He said he had to talk to you."

Peggy frowned. "Why didn't you call me?"

Her sister folded her arms across her chest. "Because I thought you wanted some time to get your head together. I didn't want you to come rushing back here. You said you needed time away, and I wanted you to have that time without him being there to cloud your judgment."

"Did he say where he was staying?"

Jeff touched Peggy's arm and startled her. "What?" she said, her voice tight. "Sorry."

"Do you think it's a good idea seeing him so soon?"

"I don't know." Peggy jumped to her feet.

"Would you really consider seeing him after what he's done?" Iris asked. "I thought you wanted to move on."

Peggy frowned at her sister. "I do, I did, but…"

"But what, love," Jeff asked. "You know what will happen if you see him now. You'll buckle under the strain and let him talk you into going back to the States with him. And then what?"

Peggy paced, chewing on her bottom lip.

Jeff stood up, walked over to her and stopped her. "I know you still love him, but don't make any rash decisions. You deserve so much more."

"Jeff's right, Peg. You know he is. Please give it some time. Don't go running back into his arms without making him fight for you." Iris walked over and placed a supportive hand on her arm. "If that's what you want."

Peggy looked at her sister, then at Jeff and sighed. "I don't know what I want."

"Then don't rush into anything." Jeff rubbed her arm. "Promise me you'll think about it before getting in contact with him."

She gazed into Jeff's concerned eyes and sighed again. "Okay. I promise I won't do anything stupid." At least she hoped she wouldn't.

Thirty

Kent was bored. He'd been holed up in his hotel suite for the past two days watching the television, in-house movies and reading magazines, and was going crazy. He paced in front of the balcony window and thought about Sunday, the day he would see Peggy again. The day he would tell her how much he loved and missed her, and how much he wanted her back in his life—as his wife.

He walked across the room to the dresser, picked up the dark blue box and flipped it open. Peggy's engagement ring sparkled in the light and he lifted it out of the box and gazed at it. He knew the ring had been far bigger than she would have wanted, but he'd been trying to make a point with the size—that he knew he was in love with her and wanted to make a life-long commitment to her. He pushed the ring back into the satin, snapped the box shut and sat it on the dresser. He stared at his strained reflection in the mirror and sighed.

Would she be happy to see him? Would she listen to what he had to say this time. Give him a chance to explain what happened face to face? Kent had to convince her he'd done nothing wrong. He *had* done nothing wrong. Why hadn't she believed in him? It didn't matter now. All that mattered was getting their relationship back on track and heading back to Los Angeles to start their life together.

Yes, he'd had a reputation for being a player in the bedroom stakes, and he'd had a lot of women in his bed, something he'd been proud of once. But when he knew for sure that he was in love with Peggy all that had changed. There was no way he would have done anything to betray her trust. He'd been one hundred percent faithful. A first for him. Kent gave a heavy sigh, realizing why she hadn't believed him. How could she? He'd been a selfish, arrogant jerk, taking the people in his life for granted.

He crossed the room to the bedside table, picked up the TV remote and pressed the red button. The midday news was on. Kent sighed again, gazed at the remote control in his hand and wished he could fast forward to Sunday.

Thirty one

Saturday morning, Peggy was sitting in her dressing gown in her living room with a cup of coffee cooling next to her on the lamp table. She'd been back home for a day and was finally on her own. Her sister had returned home to her husband and kids, and Jeff had gone back to his apartment in the city the night before, leaving her alone with her confused thoughts and feelings.

She knew Kent would still be in Brisbane, somewhere. She just didn't know where. He would be staying at one of the luxury, five star hotels, as celebrities do, but which one? The Hilton? The Sofitel? The Marriott? Should she call the reception desk at each hotel to find out? No. She had promised Jeff and Iris that she wouldn't do anything impetuous. She sighed. No matter how hard she tried, she couldn't get Kent out of her mind or her heart. Damn him! She hated to admit it but she wanted to see him.

Peggy got up and took her cup out to the kitchen and poured the coffee down the drain. She wasn't feeling hungry or thirsty. She headed to her room to shower and change. That might help make her feel better. If not, at least she'd feel fresher.

After a long, hot shower and a fresh change of clothes, Peggy began unpacking some of the few remaining boxes sitting in the corner of her living room. Iris had done what she could while she'd been away, but hadn't quite finished, and Peggy thought keeping busy would take her mind off her current situation. She picked up the box cutter, slit the tape on the top of a box marked 'Living room' and pulled out several books and stacked them on her bookshelf.

Time went by quickly, and Peggy managed to get all of the boxes unpacked and put away. By midday her appetite had returned and she was famished, so she wandered out to the kitchen to make some lunch.

As she gathered bread and sandwich fillings from the refrigerator the phone rang. Peggy dropped the sandwich supplies onto the kitchen table, walked across and plucked the cordless phone from its cradle on the wall. "Hello?"

"Hi, love, how are you?" It was Jeff's cheery voice on the other end of the line.

"Hi. I'm ok. I've been keeping myself busy unpacking the rest of the boxes."

"That's good. At least you'll be more comfortable with those out of the away."

Peggy sighed. "I guess you're right. It does feel better now that the clutter's gone."

"What are you doing tonight?"

"Staying in. Probably having an early night. Why?"

"I thought I might take you out for dinner, if you'd like to accompany me."

Peggy hesitated.

"This feels like déjà vu. The last time I asked you out for dinner you were feeling blue and hesitant to go."

"I know and I'm sorry. I just don't feel like going out."

"The same as last time. It'll do you good to get out. And I thought we'd keep with the déjà vu theme and go back to the Vanitas."

She enjoyed having dinner at the restaurant. The ambience was elegant and the food superb. It would give her a chance to dress up, which she didn't do all that often, and she would be in good company. Someone she knew she could trust.

"You're absolutely right. I do need to get out and enjoy myself. I can't sit around moping all the time. It certainly won't help me move on. And you are great company."

"Thank you. So it's a yes then?"

"Yes, I'd love to. What time?" She was actually smiling.

"Why don't we make it around seven?"

"I'll see you at seven then." Peggy rang off and wandered into her bedroom to peruse her wardrobe and decide what she was going to wear. It would do her good to get out of the house and away from her unsettled thoughts for awhile.

The evening had started out almost exactly the same as the night Jeff had come to take her to dinner, when Kent had left, hadn't been in touch and she was confused about the situation and her feelings. Déjà vu was right. The drive down to the Versace hotel wasn't at all uncomfortable though. Jeff was there as moral support and wasn't trying to win her back.

"You look lovely, as always," he said, glancing at her sideways as he drove toward the coast.

"Thank you. You're awfully good for my morale, you know," Peggy told him, smiling.

"Good. You deserve to be complimented. You're a beautiful woman." He reached across and squeezed her hand.

Peggy didn't mind.

"We'll be there in ten minutes. What do you plan on trying tonight?"

"Oh, I don't know. The quail was delicious the last time we were there. But I think I'll try something different this time, maybe the barramundi or John Dory. I haven't had either before."

Jeff frowned at her. "You haven't? Well then, you really must try both, if they're on the menu. I'll order one and you order the other and we'll share. How's that?"

Peggy shook her head. "No, no, I don't want you to order something you're not going to enjoy."

He smiled. "Hey, I love my seafood. I really won't mind. John Dory and barramundi are two of my favorites."

"Well, if you don't mind. Okay then, I'd love to try both."

Peggy felt so much better already, and knew she'd have a lovely evening with Jeff.

Thirty two

Kent had had enough of the television, the in-house movies and the various copies of tabloids, quarterly women's magazines and financial journals. He was going nuts cooped up in his suite. He paced the length of his bedroom several times, considering his options, before deciding he had to get out of there for a while.

He rushed into the walk-in robe and rummaged through the clothes that had been hung away by housekeeping staff, looking for his hooded, charcoal gray jacket. When he found it he threw it on, zipped it up and pulled on the hood. If he was going out for a walk, he needed to be incognito. No one knew he was in the country and that's the way he wanted to keep it.

The chill night air ran cold fingers over his shaved face as he slipped, unrecognized, out of the lobby doors, through the car park and onto Seaworld Drive. He wished he could jump into his rental car and drive to Peggy's tonight, but he had to do it right this time. No mistakes.

As he stalked along the street toward an all night café he wondered how he would be greeted when Peggy opened the door to find him standing on her front porch.

He hoped she would want to listen to what he had to say. To hear the *truth*. He hoped he could persuade her to change her mind and give him another chance. Surely she still loved him.

The café had internet access so, after ordering a tall latté, Kent positioned himself in a dimly lit corner with his back to the other patrons and surfed the net to kill some time.

Dinner had been amazing, the food incredible and the company on an equal par. Peggy was relaxed and had even had a glass or two of Chardonnay to wash down the delicious barramundi and John Dory fillet dishes she and Jeff had shared. Now they were waiting on dessert and coffee to finish off the evening.

The conversation had not once touched on Kent and the current situation she was in, and for that she was grateful. Peggy wanted nothing to spoil the pleasant evening she was having. She didn't want to think about Kent, their relationship issues, or what he wanted to tell her. Not tonight.

Dessert looked just as delicious as dinner. Jeff chose chocolate and cinnamon meringue with brandy custard and hazelnut ice cream, while Peggy opted for Italian orange pudding with pistachio ice cream and orange syrup. Freshly brewed coffee followed, along with petites fours. The evening had been perfect and just what she'd needed.

Jeff left her for a few minutes, and when he came back to the table he handed her an apricot colored rose. "Thanks for a lovely evening," he said, leaning in and kissing her cheek.

Peggy stood up. "I should be the one thanking you. I've had a wonderful time tonight." She hooked her arm through his and they strolled casually toward the restaurant exit.

Leaving his hood on, Kent entered the lobby. He didn't want to be recognized by any of the patrons or guests, in case someone decided to let the media know he was staying at the hotel. He kept his sight on the hallway that led to his suite and strutted across the lobby. But when he reached half way he heard a female voice he thought he recognized.

When he turned in the direction of the voice he saw Peggy and Jeff coming out of the Vanitas restaurant, arm in arm. Kent felt his face grow hot with anger and took a deep breath, counted to ten and let it out before rushing across the lobby. He pushed the hood off his head as he stalked toward the pair.

"Well this looks cozy," he said, glaring at Jeff. "The minute I'm out of the picture you're moving in on my fiancé."

Peggy looked shocked. "Kent? Wait. What are you doing here?"

Kent turned his angry gaze on her. "Obviously interfering with your romantic evening. What's next a romp in bed for old time's sake?"

Jeff grabbed the actor's arm. "Hey, steady on mate…"

"*Take* your hand off me." Kent jerked out of his grasp. "And I'm not your *mate*."

"Look, Kent, you're way off."

The actor glared at him. "Am I? I don't think so. You've still got the hots for her, haven't you? Don't deny it."

Peggy stepped between them. "Kent, you have no right talking to Jeff like that. He's done nothing wrong."

"Oh, right, you mean like I have?"

"That's the reason we're not together anymore, isn't it?"

"I've done nothing wrong either, only you won't believe me or give me a chance to explain."

Guests standing and sitting around the lobby glanced across at the arguing group, and Kent pulled up his hood to keep his well-known face obscure.

Peggy gaze moved to the people in the lobby and then back to Kent. "This isn't the time or the place. Someone's bound to recognize you if we stay here much longer."

"You mean I'm putting a crimp in your plans, don't you?" He shoved his hands into the pockets of his jacket and stared into her eyes. The pain in his evident.

"No." Peggy frowned at him. "Jeff was just taking me home."

"Of course he was."

"He … Look, there's no point trying to talk about this now. You're not going to listen anyway…"

Kent turned to walk away but stopped. "You're absolutely right. There *is* no point in discussing it at all. You've obviously made your choice. Goodbye Peggy." He stalked across the lobby and disappeared into the hallway.

Peggy started after him, but Jeff grabbed her gently by the arm. "Don't chase him, love. That's what he wants you to do."

"But he thinks we…"

"I know what he thinks. Don't play into his emotional games."

Tears welled in Peggy's eyes. "I can't help it. I'm still in love with him." She swiped at the tears spilling down her cheeks and her voice broke. "He looked so hurt."

Jeff pulled her to him. "I'm sorry, love. I know it hurts."

Peggy pulled free. She knew he knew how much it hurt. "I'm sorry. I have to go to him."

Jeff nodded and sighed. "Then go."

She kissed his cheek. "Thank you. For everything."

He took her hand in his. "He doesn't know how lucky he is."

Peggy crossed the lobby and disappeared down the hallway Kent had taken. She knew where to find him.

Thirty three

K ent couldn't believe that Peggy had run back into the arms of the British journalist. She hadn't even given their breakup time to make sense. It had only been a few weeks, not long enough to start dating on the rebound.

He snatched clothes from hangers and stuffed them into his designer travel bag, admitting that he had to walk away. What else could he do? Peggy had made her choice and moved on, and he had to do the same. What a fool he'd been, letting his heart control his well-ordered life. He should *never* have gotten involved with her, *never* let himself fall in love with her, and *never* asked her to marry him.

Kent dropped his bags by the door and used the phone to pay his account by credit card. He needed to get out of this suite, with memories of their time together, go home and get his life back. As he dropped the phone into its cradle there was a knock on the door. He assumed it was the valet for his luggage. Kent crossed the room and pulled the door open without checking, then turned around and walked over to the bedroom to make sure he hadn't forgotten anything. "Would you please take my bags out to the rental car? I'll only be a minute."

Peggy stepped into the room and closed the door. "Kent?"

He swung around, surprised by the sound of her voice. "What are you doing here?" he asked. "Came to gloat at the idiot who gave his heart to you, did you?"

She crossed the living room. "No," she said, her voice quiet. "I came to talk … to listen to what you have to say."

Kent frowned. "Don't you think it's a bit late for that? You've made your choice. What more do you want from me?"

"But I haven't. I'm not with Jeff. He asked me to dinner to cheer me up because I was miserable."

Kent's frown softened. "Why?"

Peggy stepped closer and touched his arm. "Because I miss you."

He stared into her eyes, his expression hardening again. "Why would you miss me when you were so convinced I cheated on you?"

She sighed. "I realize I wasn't fair to you. I should've listened to what you had to say before making any kind of judgment." She glanced up at him. "I made a huge mistake. I shouldn't have jumped to conclusions, should've given you the benefit of the doubt. I should've believed in you. *I'm sorry*."

Kent's stern gaze remained on her. "What makes you think I want an apology?"

Peggy's focus moved to the carpet, tears stinging her eyes. "I hoped you would. I am so sorry. What more can I say?"

"Nothing." He moved past her, crossed the room and opened the door. "You should go. I have to get to the airport."

She rushed over to him. "Kent, please don't leave. Let's talk about this."

"What's left to say? You believed I cheated on you and now you've cheated on me, so let's call it even." He motioned for her to step out of the suite. She did. "Have a nice life." And with that said, he closed the door in her face.

Peggy stood outside and stared at the door in disbelief, tears spilling down her cheeks. Kent had been so cruel. She knew he was hurting, and wanted her to feel the same amount of pain. Well he had successfully accomplished that. Her heart was aching so badly it felt as though it would explode in her chest. She turned and hurried along the hall toward the lobby, barely able to see where she was going. As she got closer, she noticed Jeff sitting on a seat near the piano.

He sprang to his feet when she reached him. "What happened, love?"

Peggy fell into his arms and sobbed. Her heart breaking.

Jeff opened Peggy's front door and helped her inside. He sat her in an armchair, then went into the kitchen to boil the kettle. He made her a cup of tea, brought it in to her and sat down in the armchair opposite.

Peggy set the cup down on the table beside her and gazed at him. "I don't understand what went wrong. Kent came all this way to win me back and …"

"He was angry, love. Once he's had time to cool down and think things through he'll call."

She shook her head and gave a heavy sigh. "No, I don't think so. I think we've hurt each other way too much to be able to work through it."

Jeff reached across and touched her hand. "Is there anything I can do to help?"

Peggy looked at him through tear-filled eyes. "There's nothing anyone can do. My apology made no impression at all. He'll never forgive me for not believing in him and I can't blame him."

The tears spilled and Jeff reached for her and held her close, stroking her hair.

It was late and Peggy was exhausted. She appreciated Jeff being there for her, but she needed some time alone. She eased herself out of his comforting embrace and looked up at his concerned face.

"Thank you for waiting tonight. I don't know what I would have done if you hadn't been there."

Jeff touched her chin and smiled. "No need, love. I'm always here if you need me. I hope you know that."

She nodded. "Yes, of course I do."

He frowned at her. "But you'd like me to go?"

"I just need some time alone. I hope you understand."

Jeff sighed. "I do." He rubbed her arm. "I'll see you tomorrow?"

"Absolutely." She walked him to the door and he kissed her cheek before stepping outside.

"You're sure you want to be alone? I could camp out on the sofa."

Peggy nodded. "I'm sure. I need to try and get some sleep. I'm totally wrecked."

"Okay then. I'll call you in the morning."

"Not too early please, I plan to sleep in, if I can. It's 11.30 already."

He headed down the path. "I'll give you a call round midday."

She waved and closed the door.

Peggy tossed and turned and couldn't get comfortable. Every time she closed her eyes Kent's hurt expression appeared in her head. Could he really believe she had gone running back to Jeff? She cared for Jeff very much, but she was in love with Kent and nothing was about to change that.

She turned over, glanced at the time and sighed. Kent would be boarding his flight to LA soon, and she would never see him again.

Peggy flopped onto her back and stared at the ceiling. She needed to stop thinking about him and try to get some sleep. But how could she sleep, knowing Kent was about to leave her life forever.

Thirty four

Kent's feeling of angry frustration grew as he sat in the First Class departure lounge and gazed out of the window at the well-lit tarmac and the massive Qantas 747 jumbo jet waiting to take him home. How could he have been so stupid? What the hell had he been thinking, traveling all this way in the hope to reconcile with Peggy? This was new territory for him, something he'd never experienced before. He had *never* been *in love* before. Man, she'd really done one hell of a number on his heart. She had wounded it beyond repair. What was he supposed to do now?

The boarding call for his flight to Los Angeles echoed over the PA. Another direct flight. He wanted to get home as fast as he could, and try to escape the painful memories he knew would remain with him for a long time.

He gazed around the lounge, hoping (somewhere deep inside him) that Peggy would come running through the doors calling for him to wait. But that didn't happen. He picked up his flight bag and headed toward the door to the boarding ramp.

As he handed his boarding pass to the attendant he heard someone call his name. Kent turned around and stepped out of the line. "What are you doing here?"

Jeff rushed over to him, took him by the arm and moved him to one side, away from prying eyes and ears. "Do you really want to do this? Peggy loves you."

Kent shrugged out of Jeff's grasp. "Look, pal, this is none of your business. Just leave it alone."

"You might be able to fool yourself and hurt her the way you did back at the hotel, and believe me you've hurt her more than you could ever know, but once you get on that plane there'll be no turning back. Is that what you really want? If you have any feelings left for her at all you'll make the decision to stay and talk to her. You owe her that much."

Kent dropped his bag onto a seat and folded his arms across his chest. "Why should you care? This whole situation would be the perfect opportunity for you to win her back, wouldn't it? You're still in love with her, aren't you?"

Jeff glanced out the window, then looked Kent straight in the eyes. "Okay, yes, you got me. I'm still in love with her. But it's because I love her that I'm trying to help you realize she's the best thing that ever happened to you. You owe it to her to try and work this out."

Kent frowned. "I don't understand you. You love her, but you're prepared to help me…"

The final boarding call came over the PA.

Kent glanced across at the young, female attendant standing at the door waiting for him to make his way to the plane, then looked at Jeff. "I have to go." He picked up his bag, slung it over his shoulder and headed to the boarding ramp.

Jeff called after him. "You do realize you're making the biggest mistake of your life, don't you?"

The actor didn't look back. He disappeared through the door, heading for the plane.

Thirty five

Peggy was awakened by the sound of knocking on her front door. She opened her eyes and gazed sleepily at her bedside clock. The luminous green numerals blurred together and she couldn't make out what time it was. She breathed a huffy sigh, sat up, snatched the clock off the bedside table and brought it up to her face. 8:05 a.m. She slid the clock into place, flung the covers back and stumbled out of bed. "Just a minute."

She threw on her dressing gown and padded barefoot out to the living room. Jeff said he'd call at noon, was he going to get an ear full when she opened the door. Peggy unlocked the deadbolt and slid the chain from the security lock. As she swung the door open she said, "It's only eight o'clock. I thought you were going to call me before you came over."

"I would have, only I thought it would be better to talk to you in person," Kent said, standing at the door with his hands tucked in the front pocket of his jeans.

Peggy did a double take. She couldn't believe he was at her door. She opened her mouth but no sound came out.

"May I come in?"

She nodded and stepped aside.

Kent walked through the door and stopped. He stood looking down at her. "Are you going to close the door?"

Peggy nodded again without uttering a word and pushed the door shut.

Kent gazed around her living room. "Nice place."

Peggy wrapped her dressing gown around her and shuffled past him. "Thanks. Um, have a seat. I'll go get dressed."

"Don't bother on my account." He eased his six feet one inch frame into her favorite armchair by the window and gazed outside.

Peggy rushed into her room and closed the door. She realized she'd been holding her breath and let it out in a long rush. Kent was in her living room! She never expected to see him again. Her heart was racing.

She paced her room.

"Get a grip, woman. Breathe, just breathe," she counseled.

All she could comprehend was that Kent was sitting in her living room. He was here. He'd come to talk. Come to work things out. He still loved her.

She sighed, a broad smile spreading across her face.

What was she going to wear? It didn't matter. Yes it did. No, it didn't.

Peggy threw on a pair of jeans and a turquoise colored T-shirt, ran a brush through her hair, sprayed on some *J'adore* perfume and opened the bedroom door. No time for makeup.

Kent wasn't there.

Peggy gazed around the room. She wandered across the living room and peered through the kitchen doorway. "Kent?"

She entered the kitchen and found him in her walk-in pantry. "What are you doing?" She stood at the open door.

He turned around with an armful of ingredients. "Talking always works better over food. I thought I'd make my mom's pancakes. Do you have any maple syrup?"

She pointed up, confused.

Kent's gaze followed her direction. "Ah, there it is." He plucked the bottle from the top shelf and came out of the pantry.

Peggy felt disoriented. Was she dreaming again?

Thirty six

While Kent made pancakes, Peggy brewed the coffee. She knew he didn't drink tea and hated the 'instant stuff'. Neither of them spoke during the preparation process, and she wondered what Kent would say when they finally sat down at the table to eat—and talk.

Her stomach did a nervous flip.

Kent gazed across at her and held out his hand. "Plate please."

Peggy picked up a plate from off the table and handed it to him. "Those smell wonderful."

"Thanks. My mom is a connoisseur when it comes to food preparation. She taught me everything I know about food and cooking." He passed her the plate. "Can I have the other plate thanks?"

She set the plate on the table and handed Kent the empty one.

"Sit. Eat. Don't let them get cold." He scooped the last four pancakes off the grill and brought the plate to the table.

Peggy couldn't help but get a feeling of déjà vu. They'd almost had the exact same conversation in her dream at the Versace hotel. It seemed so long ago now.

Kent sat opposite her and dropped a curl of butter onto his pancakes and poured maple syrup over them. He passed the syrup to her. "You can't eat pancakes without this."

"Thanks." She poured syrup over the melted butter on her pancakes.

"Oh, the coffee," Peggy said, about to get up.

Kent touched her arm. "I'll get it." He got up, crossed the kitchen to the coffee maker, poured two mugs and brought them back to the table. He set one down in front of her then sat down and took a cautious sip of his. "Great coffee."

She gave an unsure smile. "You're recipe."

They both ate in silence for a time, enjoying the food.

Peggy also enjoyed having Kent in her kitchen. It had been a while since they'd been together, apart from the embarrassing argument at the hotel, but that didn't matter now.

Kent set his knife and fork down and looked at her. "Peggy?"

She put her knife and fork on her plate and gazed into his beautiful, chocolate brown eyes. "Yes?"

He sighed. "I'm sorry about the incident at the hotel last night. I was hurt … and angry. I had no right saying those things to you. It was wrong of me."

Tears stung Peggy's eyes and she blinked them back. "I am so sorry for everything, Kent. I've been so miserable without you. I wish I could take back all the things I said to you when I saw those pictures. I should have known better."

Kent leaned back in his chair and folded his arms across his chest. "Yes, you should have." He sighed. "But I can understand why you didn't. I did have a reputation, and it was common knowledge."

Peggy stood up.

Kent stood up.

"There's no excuse, I should've believed you." She stepped closer.

"Yeah, you should have." He stepped closer.

"Can you ever forgive me?" She took another step.

"I don't know." He took another step. "I guess I can try."

"I love you so much." She reached up and brushed stray strands of his hair from his face.

He took her hand and kissed the palm. "I love you, too."

They fell into each other's arms, the passionate kiss lasting a long time.

When it ended, Peggy leaned against his chest and asked, "What changed your mind about leaving?"

Kent stroked her hair. "You wouldn't believe me if I told you."

Peggy glanced up at him. "Try me."

He gave her a cheeky smile. "I was hoping you'd say that." Kent swept her into his arms and carried her into the bedroom. He lowered her onto the bed, unbuttoned his shirt and threw it on the floor then climbed over her. Peggy sighed as he eased her up off the bed, peeled off her T-shirt, dropped it onto the floor and trailed kisses up her stomach to her neck and nuzzled her ear. She was in heaven.

Kent stopped kissing her, reached into the front pocket of his jeans and pulled out the tiny, dark blue box. He flipped it open, slid the diamond ring from the satin and held it between his fingers. He pushed the box onto the bedside table and lifted Peggy's left hand.

"Before we go any further there's something I want to ask you, *again*." He slipped the ring onto her finger and said, "Will you marry me?"

Tears filled Peggy's eyes and she leaned up, pulled him to her and held him tight, never wanting to let him go ever again. "Yes," a tiny sob stuck in her throat, "of course I will." The slow kiss between them was filled with longing.

Kent made slow, easy love to her. The kind he had made to her the first time, when he'd been in the plaster cast. He'd played her body like a finely-tuned instrument and brought her to climax several times throughout the morning, and that was something she loved about their lovemaking. She also knew everything about his oh so perfect body, and loved giving him the pleasure he needed too. Their desire sated, they drifted off to sleep wrapped in each other's arms.

Right on midday, her phone rang and she eased her arm out from under Kent's head, slipped out of bed, took the phone into the bathroom and closed the door. "Hi, Jeff."

"Hi, love, how are you today?"

"I'm feeling incredible. Kent's here."

"Oh? Well that's good news then."

"Yes … yes it is. We've had some time to talk and we've worked things out. Isn't that wonderful?"

Jeff could hear how happy Peggy was and he wanted to be pleased for her. She deserved all the happiness in the world. "I'm happy for you, love. I'm glad he decided to come back and work things out."

"How can I ever thank you?" she said.

"What for?"

"For going to the airport and talking some sense into him. If it hadn't been for you he might have flown out and we'd never be back together. There's no way I can ever repay you."

Jeff's heart was glad, but also sad because he knew this was the end for them. "You don't have to do anything but be happy."

"We will stay friends, won't we?"

"Of course we will," Jeff assured, knowing deep down that over time they would drift apart. It was inevitable.

"I truly hope the right woman comes into your life one day. You deserve to be as happy as I am. Thank you for being there for me. You've been a wonderful friend. I have to go. Bye."

"Have a wonderful life, Peggy. You deserve it." He rang off. What more could he say?

The bathroom door opened and Kent stuck his head around. "Hey, there you are. Was that Jeff?"

"Mm hm. I told him we were back together and thanked him for going to the airport."

Kent walked naked into the bathroom. "Yeah. If it hadn't been for him, I'd be on my way back to LA."

Peggy leaned up and kissed him. "You're here and that's all that matters. We don't have to think about that now."

217

He wrapped his arms around her. "What should we be thinking about then?"

She gazed into his delicious, chocolate brown eyes and said, "Oh, I can think of plenty of things." She grabbed his hand and playfully tugged him back into the bedroom.

Kent fell onto the bed, pulled her to him and kissed her long and hard. The time they had spent apart made him realize just how much he needed her, and now that he had her in his arms again there was no way he would ever let her go.

Peggy pulled her mouth from his and stared into his loving eyes, knowing in her heart that she was finally with the man she was meant to spend the rest of her life with.

ACKNOWLEDGMENTS

The completion and publication of this book (my second) would not have been possible without the love and support of my family and friends. A special shout out to *Janelle James* for reading this novel in manuscript form and giving feedback from a romance reader's perspective. Thank you so much.